A HAZARDOUS MISSION

The 2nd moon of Jupiter has been turned into a prison planet, where for several generations robot drone ships have been dumping the scum of the universe, which are patrolled by a ring of advanced security satellites that would destroy any vessel attempting to land. After a century of research, old core samples from the ice moon revealed that the frozen oceans of Europa hold the base element for an immortality drug that can extend the human lifespan several-fold.

Now greedy military corporations race to exploit this new fountain of youth, only to discover they can't seem to disable the orbiting sentry which was programmed to guard the inmates and protect itself at all costs.

It appears the Confederation has a problem. How do they get past a self-evolving AI which has appointed itself as Warden? And furthermore, retake a planet roaming with the galaxies worst criminals who might well be immortal themselves.

Titles by Michel Savage

Faerylands Series
The Grey Forest
Soulstorm Keep
Sorrowblade
Ivory

Shadoworld Series
Shadow of the Sun
Veil of Shadows
Shadows Gate

Outlaws of Europa
Rebels of Alpha Prime

Hellbot • Battle Planet

A Couple of Zeros

Forgotten Future

Broken Mirror

Project EVE

Witchwood

MICHEL SAVAGE

Table of Contents

OUTLAWS OF EUROPA

The Grey Forest
P.O. Box 71494
Springfield, OR 97475

www.GreyForest.com

Cover art by Michel Savage

ISBN: 978-0-9719168-1-4

First Edition: December 2003

Printed in the United States of America

0 9 8 7 6 5 4 3 2 1

The Bar

Attention! Prisoners H-16 through H-28, in sixty-two days you will be deployed upon the surface of Jupiter-Six." The annoying metallic monotone voice of the security computer drilled into my head at 120 decibels, which made it slightly difficult to ignore.

Here I was, partially reclined in a narrow tube of plasti-glass, wired and strapped in for a long unpleasant ride. Fully understanding that I would be asleep for 99.98% of the trip, and I don't really mind catching up on a few winks myself, but I say 'unpleasant' because of the several gallons of greenish goo that was starting to fill my cryo-tube felt like cold cottage cheese. Sure, I was wrapped in the latest protective gear, but the damn stuff was statically charged and had a weird fuzzy sensation that pierced through my clothing, making me feel completely naked. It tickled my toes, but as it worked its way up, I winced as it reached my groin. My hands were secured and there's nothing worse than having an itch you can't scratch.

In the dim light of the ship I glanced over at my colleague stationed directly across from me, noticing that he was also staring squeamishly at the gunk filling his tube. Crap, this stuff was cold! As the cryogenic gel reached my neck, the computer cut in again.

"Upon deployment of this unit on J6, the transit vehicle will disembark. In the event of any malfunction of this transit vehicle upon your arrival at the destination coordinates or if the service unit should fail to detach from the housing of your stasis chambers," …it decided to leave a dramatic pause, "this system will initiate an emergency self destruct, and you will have ten minutes to evacuate the area. This warning will not be repeated." Oh great! So, if you're still disoriented from the revival stage, too bad, huh?

As the goop flowed up over my eyes and blurred my view of the ship around me, I began to regret ever getting involved with this whole crazy plan. I also wondered what interesting thoughts were going through the heads of the rest of my crew.

Upon topping off, the vile greenish sludge began to crystallize and I started to blackout. Well, two months is sure a long time to do nothing but think about how I got myself into this mess, only a few short weeks ago I was a normal Joe with a semi-boring life…

ಬಂಧ

"Hey, Jim, whatcha work'in on?" Sarah nudged up to my table and promptly helped herself to a seat. Sarah was cute, in a dorky kind of way, but a nice person on the inside. It was a warm day outside. Too bad I had to get caught up on this inventory list for the systems log and ended up having to bring my damn files with me on my lunch break.

"You know me... all work and no play." I winced, realizing I really didn't have much of a social life outside of the company. Sarah could see through that; I had a gut feeling that she suffered the same affliction. She was probably thinking that us social lepers should stick together, but I never let on that I much rather preferred to savor my slice of misery alone. But like I said, Sarah was a nice girl, and I'm not that much of an ogre. I guess I could take a few minutes to amuse her.

"Hey, how about coming with the gang from the Stock Dept over to the new Rocket Bar after your shift, Jimmy?" Jeeze, how could I politely decline? Hanging out with a bunch of stockroom geeks was not my idea of entertainment, and besides, crowds always made me nervous.

"The Rocket Bar, eh? Why would anyone want to call a hip upscale nightclub after some part of trashy technology that hasn't been used for over 200 years," It was more of a statement than a question.

"Come on, it'll be fun!" She immediately pulled out her holopen and wrote down the address right on top of my vid-screen. "You need a drink or two to loosen up, I'll even spot you a few credits." She smiled as she patted me on the back like I was some old hound dog trying to cough up a furball, and merrily walked away. I glanced back at her once as she boarded the elevator at the corner of the cafeteria; she was still looking at me and waved. I quickly turned away... how the hell do you erase markings from a holopen anyways?

Ӡ☽Ѽ

The bar was packed, and after a day like I had, I took Sarah up on those free drinks she had offered.

"Glad you made it... so how was your day?" Sarah always had a way of being so damn polite that I felt like a real jerk if I didn't return the kindness.

"Well, I got the inventory done and it took me an hour to figure out that holopens don't use ink." I grumbled amusingly, "I had to go down to the optics department to borrow a UV light to swipe my screen clean."

"Oh, hah, sorry about that." She giggled, "I forgot you don't have those over in the Engineering section." She just scrunched her shoulders and gave that goofy smile of hers again. I really didn't think that little of Sarah, I just kind of knew a person like her was too good for me because I didn't know how to be a good friend back.

"But thanks for the drinks. I guess I needed a break anyway." This was true in more ways than I could count.

After I got my Associates degree, I had spent the last few years trying to work my way up in the company. Aerospace was not one of my favorite hobbies to tinker with, but it sure paid the bills. With all the new waves of technology that seemed to be popping up every month and numerous colony planets that were spreading, it was a pretty damn near secure job. Just like toilet paper… it was something everyone needed to use sooner or later.

The bar was set up with displays of vintage Rocket-man movie posters and scenes from really old B flicks. The place was busy, to say the least, considering synthahol could knock you on your ass if you didn't watch your intake. This stuff was better than the original liquor though, and had the same effect but without the hangover or liver damage. Two decades ago, some idiot tried to sell synthahol that had all the flavoring but without the kick. Needless to say, the dude went bankrupt. Though by law, all synthahol was laced with (no pun intended) a cocktail of downer drugs mixed in. These were all safe of course. The intention was to keep the patrons mellow, instead of getting all high-strung and causing fights.

Unfortunately, there were other elements in our modern society that righteously got off on an artificial kick and stirring up trouble. I smelled their type the moment they walked into the bar.

They were two of your typical punk junkies, probably just here to check out a bit of lucrative territory for some underhanded narcotics sales. One of them had some weird hipster hairdo that was a fad among the lower classes. His half-shaved head left his right side completely bald, and the other with iron-flat blonde hair. Personally, I thought it looked hilarious.

His muscle was an oversized grunt wearing all black and purple leather, complete with numerous rings and useless zippers. His head was adorned with colorful tomahawk spikes that must have been so caked full of gel they would've been capable of hurting someone. Not a bad looking fellow actually, but not attractive either. The ape must have weighed at least 300 lbs, probably due to an overuse of black market steroids.

They swaggered into the bar as if they were honored guests at a ball. A few people noticed them too, and most jumped out of the way of the walking ape. Sarah and her friends didn't even notice as he approached, as they kept themselves busy gossiping about their idiotic bosses and rumors about who's dating who.

These two street punks got my immediate attention though, because of my searing hatred for all drug dealers. Most people wouldn't understand my point of view, in fact, a few decent folks still practiced recreational drugs but they were as harmless as abusing over-the-counter cold medicine. The short story is, I had a girlfriend once a long time ago. She was great, perfect even, until she got involved using some heavy crap. I did everything I could to talk her off of it, but her dealer and hardcore junkie friends frequently intervened, not wanting to lose her as a customer.

They made a few threats to me here and there, and I planned on turning them in to save my girl. The next time I saw her though, she was dead. She had suffered a cardiac arrest from an overdose. Then it all became personal. I searched everywhere, but I never did find those punks. Now I keep an unlicensed Stinger hidden in my living unit, just in case I ever ran across their ugly mugs again.

Since its initial inception over a century ago, the Confederation had done a decent job of cleaning up illegal trash across the joined nations. Sure, it had a few problems at first, I read in the history manuals about how the public revolted against the police state that had sprung up overnight and the near-decade of martial law that followed. They were almost snuffed out of existence a few times but got their act together when the politicians finally appointed a few civil liberty Reps on their board. That way, both sides could pull the strings and make informed decisions that affected all us lowly taxed-to-death civilians.

The system works quite well, but after all these years one old rule still applies; you've got to catch the bad guys first. Justice here was swift. New technology could decipher whether the suspects were lying or not, and that pretty much condemned you or set you free. No lengthy trials of the past, usually the turn around was a day or two for each perpetrator. In the beginning, the Confederation was guilty itself for abusing the technology of the time, and they decidedly executed criminals on the spot. This didn't go over too well with the public, and a few commanders in chief got dismissed from their posts as a result.

Space travel had become a norm for just about everyone, and since the overpopulated Earth didn't have much room to spare, or the fact that several city governments frowned on the idea of a penitentiary in their already overcrowded suburbs, they decided to ship the inmates somewhere else altogether; someplace far away where they could be forgotten.

This arrangement satisfied the bleeding hearts, while the Confederation was happy to accept public funding and full responsibility for the project. It was commonly suspected that they adjusted the books here and there so that a generous percentage of the prison project funds would wind up in their own coffers, but they're shady accountants did a quality job of covering that up.

The 2nd moon of Jupiter was turned into a prison planet. The High-ups called it J6, because in technical terms Europa was in fact the 6th moon, not the 2nd. Everyone but the backward minded military didn't count the first 4 minor asteroids, and typically they didn't care.

A century or so ago while interplanetary travel was still in its infancy, we decided to take a jaunt around the solar system. Mankind founded a handful of mining colonies on the Moon, Mars, Mercury, and a number of the Galilean satellites, but these puckered out after a few short decades.

Europa turned out to have a few surprises, like an atmosphere that was even more breathable than Mars, but it only extended a few hundred meters above the surface. Apparently, oxygen was seeping up through the layer of ice covering the planet. One manned exploration team even took a few years to study the frozen moon and was a convenient research and supply depot for orbiting stations studying Jupiter at the time. It was pretty much like camping at the North Pole, but God knows why any moron would want to do that.

With new alloys from the Lunar mines, a quite inexpensive and highly effective type of shielding was produced for traversing through lethal radiation belts, so getting around became that much easier. Europa became the perfect place to implement their new 'fire and forget' program of lowering their prison population on Earth to almost nil.

They also put up a brilliant self-sustaining system consisting of four sentinel satellites around the frozen moon, which was a masterpiece of machinery at its time. They would send it upgrade programs periodically, but eventually, it was considered old technology. It did its job of safeguarding the penitentiary, so the Confederation didn't see any need in spending a billion more credits to replace something that already worked.

Part of this 'crime deterrent' method, was to televise the launching of each and every prison ship bound for J6. This worked out better than expected. Get caught doing a serious felony and you would get shipped off to a big ball of ice within the week. Leaving all family, friends, warm autumn days, beach vacations, green trees, and sunny beaches behind with no chance of parole. It certainly gave a whole new meaning to putting low-life gangsters on ice.

∞

Back to the two punks at the bar… I was keeping Sarah entertained with my aloofness. She and her friends were getting a bit tipsy and equally stupid with their comments when one of them made a careless mistake.

"Hey, look at the gorilla with the cute hairdo," Claude blurted out while pointing his finger with a drink in his hand. Claude was a good friend of Sarah's, but 'Clod' as I called him, had a bad habit of saying stupid things at the worst times. This was one of them.

The huge grunt overheard him and waddled his bulk over to our table; his accomplice was only two steps behind.

"You talk'in about me?" The enormous goon grunted.

I watched Clod as he opened his mouth as if to say something, but I think Sarah elbowed him in the ribs. The smaller, lanky one, came up to brush shoulders with the agitated hulk.

"Hey Rock, no need to scare the customers… I'm sure they didn't mean no disrespect now did ya?" He asked.

Sarah's friends all shook their heads solemnly. I just bit my lip.

"This here, is Rock," giving off a dopey smile and patted the overgrown sidekick on his leathered back, "and I'm sure he wouldn't do anything to offend our customers," The punk conceded as Rock snorted in reply.

"Hey you, slick, how about some Ex, or a few caps of Yellow, just fifty credits a hit." He was staring a Clod. I was seething, but doing a good job of masking it until I decided to butt in.

"And who are you, little man?" I dared to ask.

He took a step back from me with a wry grin of amused surprise crossing his face.

"You can call me Tracey, this bar is my place for doing business. How about you pretty boy, you look like you need a couple of pops of Yellow, only seventy credits for you man."

"Seventy? I guess the price is going up by the minute," I retorted in the most monotone voice I could muster.

"It'll be eighty if you don't hurry it up and hand over your credits." Those last words of his had the edge of a threat in them. Yellow was a schoolyard drug but it could still cause brain damage, and was illegal as flashing a nun in a church. I was starting to steam at this point. This guy was trying to push his rat poison on us, and expecting me to pay for it.

"We've got other customers waiting dude, pay up and we'll walk away." Those beady little eyes and his half-bald head were getting on my nerves, plus the fact I didn't like his pushy attitude. Sarah tried to grab my arm as I leaned forward, but I just pulled away.

"Tracey, huh? I inquired as the idiot just smiled back, "It seems like your parents were expecting a girl," I smirked.

I had always had a habit of being a bit cocky with people I didn't like. Rock pushed a chair aside and took a swing at me. It connected, and I went out like a light.

Recruited

I woke up to Sarah placing a cold patch against my forehead and I could tell she had been crying. I looked around, guessing it was her place I had been dragged back to. Nice style, awfully girlie though ...but nice. The black fog in my head started to clear away, I don't remember how I got to her place, nor do I recall the moment of impact, or my limp body dropping like a stone to the bar floor. Sarah was kind enough to fill me in on the details.

"*Mmmh*, what did I miss?" I groaned. It actually hurt to speak.

I tried to prop myself up but when I turned my head to look at Sarah, a wave of pain erupted in my left ear. That goon couldn't even aim his punches, though I do remember his ham sized fist coming at me. He had struck me in the side of the head; I could feel the hot blood under my skin. It surprised me how it literally felt like it was burning. I wasn't going to complain much; realizing I could have been thrashed much worse, and it felt as if that punch was the only one he had gotten in.

"Oh, Jim, hold still," Sarah demanded softly as she gently laid me back down, "You were lucky, I can't believe you spoke to that guy like that," She seemed seriously worried over a simple punch in the head.

"He was just some punk, I don't put up with his type messing with my friends," I boasted while trying to sound brave, which was a joke at this point.

"No, no, after that guy hit you, things got much worse." Sarah put her hand to her mouth and looked away as if she was reliving the moment; she seemed more troubled than I had first thought.

"How much worse?" I dared to ask.

"Oh God, Jim," her eyes started to tear up again, "when that big guy hit you, one of the bartenders came over to help pull him away. When he told those two punks to leave, they refused. He grabbed the smaller guy to shove him out, but he pulled out an MD, and… oh, god Jim, he shot him right there in front of us!"

Holy crap, a molecular disrupter! That small time punk was carrying some big-time hardware. Guess I got lucky with that punch after all, too bad for the bartender though.

"Is he…?" I half inquired with a raised brow.

"Yes," she said softly, "those two guys ran after they fried him." An interesting choice of words, but that *was* what an MD did to living flesh.

"Are your friends okay? Sorry, Sarah, I'm really sorry." I nearly blubbered like a child, I hated feeling guilty. Sarah didn't say a word; she just nodded while wiping tears from her face. She left for a few minutes and came back with some hot tea, I had no idea what time it was.

"How did you get me here?" I asked, trying to make some polite conversation.

"Claude helped me carry you outside and he drove us here." She gave a faint smile. Well, it looks like I owe Clod one, hope he won't harp on me later about this.

"Sorry about taking you back to my place, but I couldn't open up the voice lock on your condo, with you being unconscious and all," She had a point, not even thump prints could open modern locks if the owner was passed out, those things read your pulse rate. It seemed like a good security feature for most cases. That was fine with me. Being a career bachelor, my place was a holy mess anyhow.

"Oh, um... I did have to give your name to the police when they showed up. They told me to take you to the hospital, but I took you here instead. I hope you don't mind, I remember you telling me once that you hated hospitals."

"Yeah, thanks Sarah," I flashed back. Sure, I might have had a concussion and this bleeding behind my ear hurt like hell, but I *did* hate hospitals. I always believed that was where people go to die, and I didn't have much faith in quacks despite all the modern gizmos that could assist in healing.

"What time is it, by the way?" I asked.

"Just a little past two." She grinned, slipping my empty teacup out of my hands. She got up and took it back to the kitchen. I could hear her speaking from the next room. "Would you like to spend the night here? It's really no problem," I thought I could hear a faint sign of hope in her voice, not knowing what she had in mind.

I made sure to act like I was dead asleep by the time she got back into the bedroom.

ഇ෦ൽ

I tried not to wake Sarah when the alarm went off. She had one of those fancy full-size vid-screens windows that woke you to the lapping of waves and the sounds of the ocean, pretty much programmable for anything you choose. It gave an illusionary view of a peaceful sunrise. I sat there and watched it as the food processor made me some coffee. It was certainly more relaxing than the harsh metal landscape of the city outside.

The city was nothing but towering buildings several stories above and below ground, with swarms of personal transporters screaming through the air. It was quite depressing for someone who was brought up in the rural countryside like I was. Not much of that left on Earth though. Before I slipped outside, I thought about chartering a taxi, but public transportation was free in the city. It hasn't been too crowded this past decade or so, as a sizable chunk of the population had taken jobs on distant off-planet colonies.

It was a nice change, since Earth was in a real shit-hole about fifty years ago. Every major city was so overpopulated that we began to have food shortages, which was hard to believe considering the advances in agriculture and mass-scale hydroponics. But 20 billion people worldwide were a lot of mouths to feed.

Those five decades ago, new forms of propulsion like the 'Light Drive' made travel to off-world colonies cheap and affordable. With all the overcrowded cities, people were happy as hens to trade in their little box here, in exchange for a little box under a dome on some airless planet. It didn't make much sense if you ask me.

Alpha Prime was the first stable colony founded in the Alpha Centauri quadrant since it was the first test run of our long-range light drive. It was considered by the world's scientists as our best bet of finding terrestrial life. The star system was actually over 4 light-years away, but new technology managed to bend or even break a few of Einstein's antiquated theories. Especially with cryogenic suspension for the passengers, by putting them in stasis for the trip it saved vital space on the interstellar transports for propulsion.

I heard reports that Alpha Prime was a triple star system, with two Earth-sized suns accented by a red dwarf. The first pioneers were looking for something they called a 'life zone' and they found it. As the number of stable colonies increased, a large portion of the population took off to terraform these planets and build new settlements.

With fewer people around, there were a stack of jobs to fill back on Earth, though machines replaced most of those available. The Worker Unions, as they called themselves, rallied to make sure 'real' people still had jobs. A good thing too, otherwise most corporations would run solely on robotics if they felt they could get away with it.

The transit system got me to work in a flash and I found myself with some free time on my hands before I had to be at my department, so I took a shortcut to the lavatory to clean myself up. Luckily, the punch I took didn't leave me with a black eye or worse, but I still had to walk slow and not turn my head too suddenly because of the dull throbbing pain in my left ear. I had tried that maneuver once already, and I immediately felt as if I was going to faint.

Of all people, my boss walked into the bathroom.

"Good morning Jim, you're here awfully early," He gleamed. Our supervisor was one of those clean-cut jumpsuit junkies. He was a little overweight, but at least he acted a bit friendly, if not a tad nosy. But hell, I guess that was his job.

"Morning Mr. Meyers, I was uh, just catching up on some work I wanted to get done today." Hoping that sounded thrifty of me.

"Good, good…" he looked off while draining himself at the urinal. After he finished and cleaned his hands under the sonic dispenser, he turned back to me on his way out the door.

"Oh Jim, if you wouldn't mind dropping by my office before lunch, an investigator mentioned he would like to speak with you about an urgent matter. You can take the call in my waiting room when you arrive, the secretary will be expecting you." He waltzed out the door before I could catch the look on his face, so I just stood there glaring at my reflection in the mirror.

"Well, this should be interesting," I mumbled to myself.

೮೦೦೪

A few hours into my shift, I decided to drop by Mr. Meyers' office to take that call. I had never been in trouble with the law, well, except for that one vigilante hero thing I did when I was just a kid. But it was my understanding they still erased records for incidents when you're a minor. Well, at least that's what they tell us ignorant civilians.

Meyer's office was pretty simple, in an art deco kind of way. Sharp arcs of brushed metal graced the room, while his desk was hidden behind a layer of frosted glass. I was sure it was one of those types of monochrome displays that allowed one to see out, but no one to see in.

I told the secretary my full name, ID number, and department sector and she kindly invited me to take the call at a private vid-screen at the other side of the room. I didn't like the fact that the screen conveniently faced the frosted glass to his office, so I tried to gracefully position myself in the seat and hunched over the screen. I attempted to appear as if I was leaning, but was pretty sure it came off looking as an awfully uncomfortable pose to the secretary as she signaled to me that my call was being connected.

The screen flashed to life, and a surly middle-aged man in a casual gray uniform was staring back at me.

"Good morning sir, are you James William Graham?" he asked politely.

"Uh, yes… that's me," I responded like an idiot, trying not to look nervous.

"Mr. Graham, could you please put your hand on the image scanner to verify your ID, please." He asked, an I did so as the screen momentarily shifted to the generic outline of a palm print; he came back on a second later.

"Thank you, Mr. Graham. I apologize for disturbing you at work, but we had a report of a serious incident at a location you were visiting last night, and understand you were assaulted. I would have taken your statement last night but you never checked in at the local hospital." He finished plainly.

"Um, yeah, sorry about that. I, uh..." I stammered while trying to lower my voice so my boss wouldn't overhear, "I was knocked unconscious, and it was actually one of my coworkers who took me home."

"One of our officers attempted to reach you at your living unit, but did not find you at that location," He responded with a raised brow.

"Oh um, she… uh, they took me back to her ...I mean, *their* place. *Hmm*, sorry," I blurted and was really starting to sound like a dunce, this whole thing started to get me nervous about that unlicensed weapon I had stashed in my condo. It wasn't illegal, but not having it registered might have me written up on some report with possibly a whole slew of unseen consequences; or maybe I was just getting all wired up over nothing. Still, to my discomfort, the investigator seemed to be recording this down, and finally turned his attention back to me.

"I don't know if you are aware of it or not Mr. Graham, but the perpetrators who assaulted you last night also committed a murder with a banned weapon. It is important to the case if you could immediately come down to the precinct in section 12 of the G sector. I will notify your employer to release you for the day, you will receive full payment for your days shift of course… and your cooperation would be appreciated."

I just nodded at him, and was about to say; "Yeah, sure, no problem," or something equally stupid, when the screen suddenly went blank. I glanced over to the secretary, who I guessed was busy responding to the formal request of the officer. When she was finished, she handed me a transfer card along with one of her fake smiles.

"You have been excused for the day Mr. Graham, your work assignment for this afternoon will be extended another day. Here is the address of your appointment with the local Confederation Office."

I tried not to look too obvious as I flashed a nervous glance back at that wide frosted glass wall while I walked out the door, and was only just a few steps down the hall when I began wishing I hadn't done that.

ഓറ

Time flew by on my way to the station, but I was far more relaxed when I finally got there. I didn't have a grudge against the military but these guys in uniform still made me a bit edgy, I guess it was from all the trumped-up rumors I had heard from time to time about the Confederation police.

I passed through their retro-scanner and into the main office. Gave my name, did the whole hand scan thing again just for kicks, and was led into a waiting room. Some guy briefly glanced at me through the door window for a split second, and then disappeared. I was guessing it was the same fellow that strolled into my waiting room ten minutes later. However, it wasn't the same officer who I talked to during my first call.

"Good afternoon Mr. Graham." he came over to shake my hand as a silver orb floated into the room behind him.

"My name is Lt. Charles, I took over this case from Investigator Rollins whom you spoke with this morning." He graciously plopped down in the seat across the table as the orb disappeared behind me. I had never seen one of these gadgets in person; supposedly they could do all sorts of cool stuff, but were police issue only. I was still a bit wary as it hummed about the room.

"Don't mind the ball, Jim; it's just a standard recorder for these types of conferences." He gave a quick smile and set about flipping through some digital files on his clipboard. While he was doing that, a black metal rod arose from the middle of the table and a hologram buzzed into life directly above it.

"This won't take long, Jim… may I call you Jim?"

"Sure." This guy caught me off guard with his friendly manner. I guess I had been expecting a dark room with a spotlight shined in my face.

"Sorry for the personal question, but have you taken a shower, or used a sonic unit since your visit to the club… ah, Rockets, last night?" He asked as he read the file and glanced back at me.

"No, um, actually, I kind of just washed up a bit when I got to work this morning." He seemed satisfied with that answer and motioned to the orb.

"Lucky break for us then; I understand you were assaulted last night, could you tell me where you were struck please, and if the assailant was wearing gloves perhaps?" I recounted the whole story about the incident at the bar, and gave him... well, actually gave 'the ball' permission to scan the left side of my head for DNA samples, as they were looking for skin flakes from the grunt who clobbered me. Only a moment later the guys face appeared in the hologram on the table.

"Yeah, that's him. The other guy didn't touch me though; he was just trying to push some drugs on us." I tried to get comfortable in the little wire chair, and my ear was still throbbing a bit. I didn't want him to notice and order me to see a doctor, so I tried my damnedest not to look distracted.

Apparently, they also had the other goon on file, because the hologram changed to show that other punk, 'Tracey', same scrawny face, but with a different haircut.

"Thank you for your time, Jim. Your testimony will be included in the Tribunal hearing when these two felons are caught," He switched off his digital clipboard and ordered the orb to leave the room. I was waiting for him to tell me that was all, shake my hand goodbye or some other cue to let me go on my merry little way, but he just kicked his feet up on the table and lit a cigarette. So of course, I squirmed accordingly.

"You sure have grown up, Jim." He stated, while this turn of the conversation caught me off guard, "Last time I saw you, you were just a tot."

"Were you..?" I began to inquire, because this guy didn't look familiar to me in the least.

"Yes, I was a friend of your fathers. You have my condolences, he was a good man," He offered while I just nodded grimly in reply.

It had been nearly a decade since my mother, father, and sister died, it was one of those freak accidents. They were on vacation while I was away at the Academy during my freshman year. One of the grav-discs on their personal transporter had malfunctioned and sent them into an uncontrolled dive to the ground. They were killed on impact, and I've been on my own ever since.

"So I understand you took up Aeronautics like your father," The lieutenant grinned.

"Yeah, I'm still just an intern in the Engineering Dept at my company, but I should be upgraded to a real post by the end of the year," I added in a hopeful tone, since I could hardly get by on the dirt wages I was making as an intern.

"Well, if you're interested Jim, I have a little project that could make you some extra credits, probably enough to pay off your academic loans and a tidy sum left over to last you a while. If you accept, it may even get you a prime position in the Confederation designing starships." He offered while his comment got my attention.

The lieutenant asked me to meet him later that evening at his personal office in the H sector. I had the rest of the afternoon off, so I went home to get some rest and to make sure my Stinger was thoroughly hidden, just in case. The murder at that bar made the nightly news, but for some reason they didn't show the faces of those two thugs, which didn't make much sense to me at all. Well, I wasn't gonna play smart-ass again with a guy who liked to wave around a disruptor like it was a toy. I thought it would be prudent to go incognito for the night, and put on a beret and a pair of shades before I left my condo.

I met Charlie in his office and apologized for being a little late for getting lost. For a guy of his position, his office was quite modest. I had expected something fancy perhaps, but it was as ordinary as oatmeal.

The lieutenant had a few surprises in store for me. I had

to ask for a stiff drink just to help me take it all in. First off, it didn't make sense why he would want someone as green as me to help him with a confidential project, but the six digit number in credits he mentioned quickly shut me up and got me listening.

Before we started, he made me give my thumbprint & retinal on a confidentiality agreement. Charles threw some files at me, and it took most of the evening to get the story straight.

It seemed like our Confederation had more internal problems than the media let onto. The fiasco with the military tribunals and cold-blooded executions a century ago had left a permanent scar on their reputation. When the military boys initiated the J6 project, they had a bunch of liberals hovering around them like hawks, making sure the inmates were treated civilly, etc, etc.

Sending the major offenders off-planet was pretty harsh as it was, considering there was no chance of parole, which threw any form of rehabilitation out the window. Several years before that, they made numerous attempts to wipe the memories of repeat offenders, but it ended with disastrous results. That botched experiment only left the government responsible for a sizable number of slobbering zombies that were nothing more than walking vegetables, a debacle they had a hard time keeping under wraps. After they swept that one under the carpet, they got a good portion of the public to vote for an off-world penitentiary. This is where the Confederation took charge and started the SENTRY Project on Europa.

They got some clever programmers to develop a self-sustaining computer complete with artificial intelligence. It was quite a decent piece of machinery for its day and age, using hardware far ahead of its time. Decade upon decade of new technology eventually made the system seem like it was small potatoes, but its price tag for replacement kept it from being shelved, so they just sent it upgrade software from time to time. During all this, Earth kept on shipping out its hostile inmates via robotic shuttles periodically. The Sentry worked by scanning these incoming ships for life forms and would compare it with its existing database.

Now, of course, all the prisoners were put into cryo-stasis for the two-month journey to the ball of ice, and the satellite would monitor their vital signs to make sure everyone was comatose before letting the ship set down. The drone ships then detached their cargo, and promptly set off back to Earth to pick up another load of felons.

At the time this whole project was dreamed up, laser propulsion and light drives had not yet been invented, and it was sensible for a robotic drone to pilot the craft. It was conventionally designed, so that if by any remote chance a group of prisoners should manage to hijack a shuttle and try and make an escape, they would be hard-pressed to find a cockpit, flight controls, or even any type of life support system for them to utilize. For security purposes, it was engineered to work in this manner.

Since the drone ships had very little wear and tear, the Confederation took the age-old stance of '*if it ain't broke, don't fix it*' attitude, so the transports were never upgraded to install them with modern light drives.

The shocker of the evening came when the lieutenant's mood became notably serious about what he was disclosing, and that the information he was divulging was not to leave his office. It seemed the Confederation had a few interstellar problems as it were. In the past few decades, several billion people had been leaving to build new colonies in space, many of which had broken ties with mother Earth, and thus had refused to pay taxes accordingly.

This type of scenario has been played throughout human history… so much for the free revenue. So as it was, the Confederation didn't have much choice but to let these colonies separate into their own entities. The Earth government just didn't have the resources to 'hunt them down and make them pay' as it was. This type of police action would have also had long-reaching political consequences if they had attempted such folly.

Now the belt on the Confederations budget had been squeezed even tighter since it was receiving far less funding from this lost revenue. To bring this situation into perspective, the upper officials were used to living high on the hog, to say the least. So, the extra credits had to come out of somewhere, and their first easy target was the J6 enterprise.

Only a few decades into the project, these councilmen began to dip their greedy little paws into the funds. It was convenient since nobody really checked up on the prisoners or its records very closely. As long as they fed the public reports that the inmates arrived in good health, nobody really seemed to care about what happened to them afterward.

I guess earth society was just oblivious to the facts and thought the convicts were merrily building snowmen while self-repenting over their bad deeds. However, the Confederation Council had a more realistic idea about what was going on there. All along, their stringent plan was that these inmates would eventually kill each other off in a desperate fight for survival on the bleak moon. Of Course, this news was never brought into the public forum, and any reference to their health and welfare was immediately sacked by a swarm of PR agents whose job was to sugar-coat the facts till your ears would bleed.

When the program began, inmates where set down in random sectors by the robotic transports along with a fully sustainable shelter unit. These same drone ships would also drop food shipments upon every visit. As the years passed, the greedy weasels in the upper ranks of the military kept dipping their sticky hands into the coffers. As a result, the food shipments for the prisoners incarcerated on Jupiter's moon began to dwindle sharply. Currently, the drone shipments left their inmates with only a one-month supply of rations... just one month! This was basically sending these felons to their death, and the fight for survival would cross a very thin line.

Worse yet, when each high official in office embezzled funds, they sent along programming data to the Sentry which would otherwise report the loss of weight per transport volume back to them... transmitted information they didn't want noticed. To keep from getting caught, they made sure the method of data transfer would be completely irreversible.

So a lot of fat old Generals enjoyed a very cozy retirement, smiling all the while with the thought of all those inmates on J6 starving to death and killing each other off for their meager rations. Needless to say, if this information ever became public knowledge, in its current weakened state, the Confederation Corps would be completely dismantled by exposure of this scandal.

I spent a long time studying the files, documented data (which was sparse), and finally got to the question of why he needed me. After Lt. Charles had a few drinks, he finally managed to get to the meat of the subject.

The last visit of civilian personnel on Europa was a scientific survey team that was stationed there over a century ago. The story was; they were skipping along the Galilean satellites scouting for base metals and the sort for a handful of mining corporations. The filed reports had stated they didn't find anything useful, as they confirmed Europa was a planet-wide frozen ocean more than 50 kilometers deep. This information apparently didn't catch the discerning attention of the private mining conglomerates or the direction of their limited resources.

The only thing special about the ice moon was that it did have some minor bacteria readings, but nothing to get really excited about. Their major find was about its semi-breathable atmosphere, but this was the only novelty of that dead ice world.

As it so happens, while this survey crew did its planet-hopping, things got misplaced during the long trek, and an item or two were never tagged, a few records lost, etc, etc. It turns out that the core samples they took from the ice during their visit to Europa had been stored in a deep freeze locker at one of their corporate branches. With the progress in science we've had over the past century, for the first time these ice samples actually got a thorough scan and were properly analyzed.

Since the original team was only looking for ore traces, they had never thought to do a full biological analysis. Well, the eggheads have been doing research tests for the past few years and they discovered that trace samples in the ice could help produce a new and highly effective youth drug. The catch was; Europa had been certified as a government penitentiary fully funded by our taxes, and thus, was public property in the legal sense.

I had to admit, the lieutenant could hold his liquor, and this sure was a lot to take in. At first, the solution sounded simple. Just relocate the prisoners to another planet, perhaps even Ganymede, since the old abandoned mining facilities there could be remodeled into a prison facility for a decent price. But then he hit me with the root of their problem, which left me puzzled.

For several embarrassing reasons he had stated, the Confederation had to be the first one to get there... if not just to clean up their mess, then for posterity's sake.

Lt. Charles mentioned that he needed someone with my skills and background experience in flight data in other-than-earth atmospheres, and how their current Starcraft could be altered to accommodate the mass transfer of prisoners to another location. He also inquired if I might be able to alter the robot drone ships to possibly make them flyable by a live pilot. Charlie then reluctantly mentioned a certain incident with a reconnaissance vessel the Council had sent out about two weeks ago, which actually took less than a week to reach the ice moon using our modern low-scale light drive.

As the logs go, the manned ship had approached J6 and gave the Sentry its data command to let them land. After a series of confusing security protocols sent by the orbital had kept bombarding their onboard systems, they finally decided to just turn the damn thing off. So they sent the code to disable the ring of satellites and promptly proceeded to scout the planet for a viable landing site.

"And then what happened?" I inquired, expecting some sort of plain answer. Charlie put down his empty glass, then unexpectedly picked it up again and threw it to the floor where it smashed into shards.

"Not a God-damn thing!" I could tell he was drunk

now as he grudgingly kicked aside the broken glass on the floor in disgust. "We got a two-second mayday from them, only *two seconds* ...dammit! There were over three hundred trained soldiers aboard that ship!" I didn't get it,

"Did they have a major malfunction, was there any data forwarded from their distress signal?" I asked, trying to pry the details out of him. The lieutenant put his hand to his forehead, seemingly still distracted by something he had left unsaid.

"They're all dead, Jimmy-boy, their ship crashed on the surface," He muttered, the booze had effectively softened up his stout character. The cocktail of downers had taken their time to finally kick in.

"But how could that be? Our modern starships have automated emergency landing programs built-in; escape pods, orbiting boosters, safeguards and..." I began to spout, as being an aeronautics engineer, I knew just about everything being built into our modern star cruisers.

"No, no..." He cut in, "they crashed and burned on the surface," he finally finished. I was completely boggled by the apparent lack of emergency backup support on a multibillion-credit starship; I began to open my mouth when Charlie finished his rant, "and somehow, that damn sentinel satellite has turned itself back on."

Doc

The Lieutenant left me with a decent stipend while I worked on the project, and even issued me an official notice for an 'indefinite' leave of absence for my old job with Mr. Meyers. That must have created quite a stir; I could just imagine all the gossip that was flying around the office. Sarah had left me a few messages, and I felt guilty about not returning them, but I was going full force on this little plan Lt. Charles wanted kept under strict wraps. Personally, I didn't call her back because I couldn't think of a good fib to tell her if she tried to wiggle the facts out of me about the secret project I was working on …I had always been a terrible liar.

For the first few weeks, I worked on schematics and helped redesign the Confederation transport that was supposedly going to be used on transferring the inmates off to another planetoid. All these specs were then forwarded to some unknown department. I asked Charles for an assistant or another engineer to help me on the charts but he flatly refused, stating he would not approve any additional aide in this area. It looked as though I had to earn my dough the hard way.

It was far more interesting to reconfigure the drone ships to make them operational by a human pilot. I finally worked the puzzle out by removing one of the hydrogen cells, which would leave just barely enough legroom for a pilot. But when I mentioned that there was hardly enough space for the oxygen tholus needed for an extended flight in space, Charlie didn't seem terribly concerned, which I found rather odd.

Only after I was bold enough to press him about the lack of sufficient life support did he tell me that it wasn't necessary since a refitted ship would only need to get to Europa's celestial neighbor, Ganymede. But even after working out the details in my office the numbers still didn't fit as these droid ships still used the old booster technology. I estimated that any pilot trying to fly a drone ship from Europa would still asphyxiate by the time he got to the next moon. There just wasn't an adequate amount of room within the hull for a pilot *and* a full array of life support gear, without removing equipment necessary to keep the entire flight system operational. The Lieutenant's evasive answers left me at a loss; I must have gotten so obviously frustrated that he finally assigned me to another department.

One morning I was introduced to a biological scientist named Dr. Brendan, who had seemed to be working just as feverishly on some old research data while I had been slaving away on my blueprints. He also mentioned that he had been forced to work alone until he too had run into a snag, and that's when the Lieutenant had shoved the two of us together. I certainly had a lot of questions for the Doctor.

"I don't understand what the whole plan is, but from what you're working on, I would guess that the Confederation might be trying to send in one man on some undercover operation... for whatever reason," Brendan suggested with a shrug. He was your typical nerd type, tall with dirty blonde hair, and had a quirky way of working with his notes posted everywhere. He spoke to himself a lot, which made me think he must be used to working alone on late night shifts.

"I'm not sure; Charlie never really elaborated on their

next plan of action," I replied, which was a fact that kept me up late at night, "How about you fill me in on this 'youth drug' thing." I managed to inquire.

"Well," he began, scratching his head in a way I would later find to be a constant habit of his, "the bio-samples in the ice were stored in super deep freeze containment for well over a century. This had unknown effects on the biological specimens inside," He replied, and it quickly became apparent that Dr. Brendan had a habit of talking with his hands.

"The bacteria appeared to have died from the lack of solar light, but the ice core itself seemed to contain a peculiar crystalline structure at a subatomic level," He formed his hands as if there were an invisible sculpture of what he was talking about in the air in front of us.

"Uh, keep it in layman's terms if you would Doc," I urged him, as I was figuring this was going to take a while. He stuck his finger up in the air as though he had just come up with a brilliant idea, and I almost expected a lightbulb to appear above his head. He grabbed a remote and punched in some information, which promptly displayed on the vid-screen in front of us. It showed a cracked billiard ball of a planet.

"This is J6, pretty plain looking, eh?" he spouted.

"Yeah, a skiers paradise," I replied sarcastically, he hadn't grabbed my attention yet with this news.

"Well, actually not." he retorted, "Those cracks and grooves you see are actually a result of surface tension, pseudo-tectonic movements within the ice cap itself," He corrected, and I had to give him that roll out of the corner of my eyes to remind him to keep the dialog simple. "Oh well, what I mean is that most areas on Europa are fairly flat, with only large expanses of ice fields. The few grooves you see here are only a hundred meters high at their maximum point… which is pretty lousy for skiing," he smiled back; then gave his head a quick itch again, "Take a closer look Jim, and tell me what you see," Brendan requested, so I stepped forward and studied the screen, though honestly I still didn't get it, so I shook my head back at him.

"Ok, tell me what you *don't* see," He instructed. The Doc was leading up to something, but I was never really into planetary study, that sort of thing just didn't tickle my interest. It was the date on the scanner that finally caught my attention with a raised brow.

"Yes, these images are quite old, but that's only because after J6 became quarantined they wouldn't allow any surveillance probes near the moon after they started shipping prisoners there," he gestured, "but that's not what I was trying to point out."

"So what are you getting at, Doc?" I was still a bit confused at exactly what it was I missed. So he flashed through all the other non-gas planets in our solar system, each of them showing vivid surface textures.

"What makes Europa such an oddity is something that has been baffling astronomers since the moon was first discovered," He went and stood beside the vid-screen as if he were giving a lecture, but I sure as heck wasn't gonna start taking notes. Then he began pointing out features that made J6 stand apart.

"As you can see, there are no craters on Europa, none! Which would be no great surprise if its oceans were liquefied, but they have been frozen over for several million years, and since its atmosphere extends only about four hundred meters above the surface, there is no chance of asteroids burning up before impacting on the surface and leaving their telltale scars." I switched the remote to do a pan scan orbit on the vid-screen, and by God, he was right!

"Sure, that's interesting and all, but what does it have to do with this drug they're producing?" I shot back.

Doc jumped about suddenly, grabbing clipboards and remotes, and shoving them under my nose with obvious excitement as if he were showing a family album.

"Our astronomers first thought those tan-colored lines that streak the entire surface were just residue sulphur emissions from Jupiter, but that theory was trashed once we had actually set down a manned probe onto the surface. It turned out that those veins were actually a unique form of bacteria that had broken through faults in the ice," He switched files in front of me like a card dealer, "Here is a close-up of the specimen and ice crystals themselves, in microns. We believe that it is this minor bacterium that is growing in vast amounts in the liquefied portion of the oceans beneath the ice."

He adjusted the scanner to go through each of the images in several spectrum's, "You see here, that the waste product of the bacteria is in both a solid and partial gas form. It's actually these bacteria that are creating the oxygen for the atmosphere, but it's this solid byproduct that can be put to medical use," he confessed. The Doc was getting overly excited at this point even though I honestly couldn't understand most of the charts he was showing me.

"So, you're saying this bacteria poop is the youth serum?" I asked with a short grin.

"No, no, no... well, ah, kind of, I mean..." he started to fuss; this guy was fun to rile, "It is this byproduct *and* the unique ice crystals combined. The tests show that it does amazing things for organic cell repair especially for the epidermis, which seems like the only bodily organ it affects completely, however, we really need some fresh samples to work with, and that's why my research tests are incomplete."

The Doctor then proceeded to explain in an array of confusing terms that I did and didn't understand. The final result was that if this stuff was filtered and processed right, and with a constant dose of this youth-juice processed from it, an individual human lifespan could be extended anywhere from two or three hundred years or so. Wow! It was no wonder the Confederation wanted to get their grubby little hands on this ice moon.

"And who knows what other kinds of curative effects it may have, that's why we need to get some fresh samples and conduct more tests," Doc conceded, before he slumped back in his chair in exhaustion as though he had just dumped an intellectual load off his shoulders for a moment before he continued, "We think this stuff is continuously growing, and that's why there are no signs of meteor craters or scarring on the Moon's surface; it's all been restored by these bacteria and crystalline growths," he finished while flashing me a clever smirk in a way that didn't befit him.

It took some time for the Doc to admit that he had also been coerced into signing a confidentiality agreement, but since we were on the same team, he figured it was alright to let me in on another little tidbit of information.

As it turned out, the Doc here was *not* the guy who made this initial discovery; otherwise, I'm sure he would be up for a Pulitzer or two. It was a private civilian company which had taken over the bankrupt exploratory corporation that had procured the original ice samples.

Some misfiled documents led to their identity, and they eventually found the untagged core specimens in a old freeze locker and had them analyzed. This surprising discovery led them to require further testing if they were going to dump more of their limited funds into extensive research and development. However, since Europa was now a prison colony controlled by the Confederation, that is who they met with first.

The Confederation council, being in a financial bind itself and seeing the economic possibilities of this, quickly locked themselves in with a private contract with the founding company and immediately placed strict secrecy on the entire project. For reasons being that they didn't want to alert the media, and secondly, because J6 'actually' belonged to the public taxpayers, and this could cause all sorts of problems with their initial plans. The Confederation had its beady little eyes on the prize and didn't want to see potentially billions of credits worth of profit wash through their hands like a sieve. So much for ethics, it was all about the money.

Once the product was acquired and processed, the founding company would present the commercial drug to the public, while handing over a sizable percentage and any kickbacks to the Council, all under the table, of course. First thing first though, they had to somehow rid themselves of the current prison population and escort them off-planet. That was the Confederation's part of the bargain. With this new wonder drug, they could again control all those segregated off-world colonies that would desire to import their unique pharmaceutical product... for a very hefty price, of course.

Well, that explained the Lieutenant's need for secrecy, and why he was in such a rush. He was probably the only division assigned to get the ball rolling on this top-secret project. I was guessing I would be hired on as a permanent agent for the Confederation after completing this project since I doubt they would let pawns like Doc and I back into the public workforce with what we knew.

As I questioned Doc about the safety of this drug, he just couldn't give a full analysis, since the lab results were inconclusive due to the age and condition of the original samples. However, he did tend to speculate on its extraction, which did surprise me a little as the process was exceedingly simple.

He had outlined a general concept, plus a few of his own analysis that he hadn't yet bothered to share with our chief. It was an outlandish theory that caught me quite off guard. The surprising prospect was, that since the byproducts of this drug were all natural elements of Europa, and if the prisoners, in fact, were living on depleted rations, that they would have no choice but to rely on their environment for vital sustenance. Simple basic things, like getting their water from the surface ice.

The Doc confessed his theory was that these same base elements used for this drug might also alter anyone living in such a habitat for an extended period of time. It was just a guess, but one he was willing to bet on.

That night, a whole lot of unpleasant thoughts ate away at my conscience. Was it possible that the prisoners who were dumped on J6 might very well be affected by their environment, and unknowingly ingesting a raw form of the youth-serum from the ice itself? If so, it would place a whole new meaning for serving a life sentence. Furthermore, this could present a real problem to the project for relocating the prisoners to an enclosed facility elsewhere, considering the inmate population rate might be far, far higher than what they had originally estimated. That is, if the prisoners hadn't really killed themselves off over the years as our Lieutenant had presumed.

Who knows, maybe every convict deported there had only survived a month or so until their food supplies ran out and they met their demise. Then the Confederation wouldn't find any inmates left alive that required transport to the newly proposed penitentiary next door on Ganymede, and save them a whole lot of grief.

If this were the case, it would conveniently make the Councils job a whole lot easier to cover up their mess. If not, then there sure would be a lot of disgruntled convicts who would have had an excessive amount of time on their hands to do nothing but brood about their revenge.

The Mission

Charles came to the office in a huff one afternoon. After the scheduled briefing, Doc and I learned that the Confederation had sent out an unmanned probe to take a few orbital shots of the wreck site of their downed reconnaissance ship. When it arrived at J6, the Sentry satellites scanned it and forwarded several requests for clearance codes. Unfortunately, the probe was just a seeing and hearing device and had no way to communicate directly with the orbiting sentinel, so when the probe got too close to the moon, it blacked out.

"What do you mean by *blacked out*?" I shook my head and waved my hands, I guess after hanging around Doc so much that I had picked up a few of his minor habits. The lieutenant was ready to oblige us with the classified information, but he also required that we had to move into private apartments assigned to us within his own building. I agreed to these conditions, finished paying off all my debts with the advance I had been given and packed my bags for my newly assigned quarters in the Council building. This may have made things more convenient, but I also felt a little rushed into the whole situation.

The next day, I was summoned into a private council chamber by Lt. Charles and met five new associates. A gorgeous woman on the opposite side of the room grabbed my attention first. It was kind of hard to miss her; she had long, snow-white hair and her fair skin was just as pale. I was guessing that she must be an albino.

Dr. Brendan was there, he was chatting over some

digital file with a skinny Asian fellow.   A bulgy
mercenary type chap was helping himself to several cups
of coffee at the small counter, just behind a conservative
looking guy in a grayish jumpsuit sitting at the large
round conference table.   At the opposite end stood
Charlie, talking under his breath in some private
conversation with a hard-looking older man in fatigues.
Lastly, there was a lady with short blonde hair, sitting
with her back to me.

The other five people mentioned were all unknown to
me, but to my utter surprise, when the blonde woman
turned around… it was Sarah.

"Howdy stranger!" She blurted out loud enough for
everyone to hear, "Over here, have a seat next to me,"
She invited while pulling out a free chair beside her. I
also noticed that she positioned it a tad closer to her own;
I gritted my teeth quietly and accepted her offer.

"Good morning Mr. Graham," Charlie started formally,
"everyone please have a seat," he took his position at the
head of the vid-screen as it flashed into life with a
display of some confusing schematics of what appeared
to be the innards of a rather chunky satellite, "I would
like to start out by introducing everyone, as you will all
be working together on this project," Charlie began on
his right, "This is Sergeant Roland." The rough-looking
man in fatigues immediately popped up to attention
almost as if he was going to salute, then gave a curt wave
of his hand and sat back down.

"Sergeant Roland will be in charge of any military
aspects of this project, he is the next in command below
me," Charlie confirmed mildly.   He then motioned
towards the hulking lump of muscles sitting the next seat
down, "And this is Roller, he will be in charge of

weapons maintenance."

Weapons, eh? A few of us in the room at that moment looked at each other in mild shock, as we had no idea what Charlie had planned. The Lieutenant continued with his introduction by pointing over to the man in gray, who was busily trying to stack his digital clipboards quietly when all our attention was drawn to him, "In command of all computer tech support is Voc."

"Um…" Was all he said, and he flashed a quick smile, which quickly disappeared as he nodded nervously to the group. Charlie then moved on to Sarah, who tilted her head and cast a wide comical grin.

"This is Sarah; she will be in charge of all your supplies. If there is anything you need, put in a request with her office," the lieutenant advised.

"Hello everyone, nice to meet you all," She hammed up with a wave. Motioning over in the direction of my chair, Charles continued.

"Everyone, this is Jim, he is our flight engineer, and will be working on all the specs on any given transport you may be using," he offered as my introduction to the group. I didn't like everyone looking at me, it made me feel like melting right there. It helped that they all nodded courteously, and I tried not to stare at the white-haired girl at the opposite end of the table when she glanced my way. Her eyes were a rich blue, which struck me, as I thought that they should be a pale pink if she were a true albino… but then, what the hell did I know?

"Next to Jim is Dr. Brendan, who is actually our biological scientist on this mission, he…" Charlie then pointed over to the Asian gentleman next to him, "and Min Li will be working closely together in their department. Mr. Li is our medical technician, and will be monitoring the crew's health during your mission."

Mission? Holy hell, what did Charlie have in mind? I almost blurted out something to interrupt him, when he then motioned over to the fair-skinned girl. She sat absolutely still with her straight white hair framing the perfect features of her face. It was at that moment when Sarah's knee bumped me under the table as if to break the spell.

"Everyone, this is Rook. She will be in charge of all communications equipment for your group," Charlie finished, and then turned to the remote at the front of his seat.   Sarah bumped me once again, whispering something like 'Oops, sorry,' but kept her knee pressed against my leg until I nonchalantly changed position in my chair. I could swear Sarah was glaring at me every time my eyes fell upon Rook.

The technical jargon about the satellite system didn't seem to make any sense to me until Voc put it out in plain words. When it was first installed, the Sentry system was comprised of four bulky orbiting satellites that worked in unison with a shared AI brain. Their exterior housing had been constructed so unconventionally to make room for the nasty little toys that had been stored inside. Old-fashioned gunpowder handguns were a thing of the past, but imagine if you will, a specially designed gun with a plutonium bullet.

Now the physical bullet itself doesn't fire, but the energy in the form of electromagnetic radiation, does. Basically, these satellites have the ability to fire off little Hydrogen bomb-equivalent bullets of energy, sending a slaughtering pulse of gamma rays that cause massive electrical disruption to anything in their path. Only at extremely close range is this type of weapon harmful to human tissue, but its super-concentrated burst wreaks havoc on anything like computers systems or stored energy cells.

Apparently, it was this defense system that was turned against their military reconnaissance ship that went down. Even with all of its advanced equipment and modern shielding, it only held out for a mere few seconds. (Such crude, but highly effective weaponry as thermonuclear devices that this satellite employed, had been banned for nearly eighty years now, but that still falls far short of the era this unfriendly SENTRY gimmick was built. In all truth, the system should have been junked twenty years after it went into operation.)

Now this news surprised me, because of the recent shielding technology that began a few generations ago. For instance, live human pilots weren't even able to approach Jupiter until a new type of shielding ore was discovered, simply because its colossal magnetosphere continuously cascaded a deadly stream of neutrons and deflected solar radiation in excess of 400,000 rads.

Now only one-tenth of one percent of that would kill anyone as dead as a doornail, and of course, to block that level of radiation, making ship hulls out of solidified lead two feet thick was impractical, to say the least. However, the new shielding incorporated into modern starships made interstellar travel possible, since it was efficient protection from thermal and magnetic radiation, but it was apparently useless against this dirty little man-made device.

All recent attempts to shut the Sentry down have failed, and had also completely annihilated a series of rather expensive equipment in the process. This was the first step Voc was set upon, but it was Roller who suggested;

'Hell, why not just blow it out of the sky?'

There were three good reasons which made this idea useless: One, any guided missile would simply be 'zapped' by the Sentry, leaving it dead in space and most likely leaving such a munitions projectile to fall to the planet. Two, calculations show that even the military's new laser and particle accelerators would have no effect at long range due to the ingenious use of alpha-particle shielding that was built into the Sentry housing. Three, the damn thing was a very expensive piece of equipment to begin with, that they would rather not destroy.

Charles admitted that they could attempt a barrage of fire to bring all four of the satellites down by force. However, should that fail - or even succeed, that could either leave a lot of dangerous bombs floating dead in space as orbital debris until gravity pulled them in to fall like a rain of hell onto the surface of the moon. Worse yet, if we did manage to get lucky enough to knock all four of those damn satellites out of orbit, whether they exploded in space or fell to the surface of Europa, the radioactive debris from their cores could contaminate the whole planet over an incalculable area and possibly destroy the bacterial ecosystem… and this was *definitely* something they did not want to happen.

They had to protect the integrity of the moon, the ice crystals, and the fragile bacteria it housed at all costs. Either that or choose to wait out the half-life of 24,000 years for the radiation from the destroyed satellite cores to die down. Not to mention the second problem we had yet to discuss.

There was also the possibility that there might be survivors from the crash of the military recon ship. Though the calculated chances where unbelievably small, it was still procedure to send in a search and rescue party out of principle. That is where we came in, on Charlie's little secret mission to felon frosty-land. Personally, I don't exactly remember volunteering for this outlandish scheme, but our promised pay for this little excursion would certainly make it worth having a look.

Part 'B' of that same problem, was that a good amount of the weapons surplus on that downed recon ship may be undamaged or in repairable condition. Remembering that there is no thick layer of atmosphere for the ship to have burned up and disintegrate, it simply just slammed into the surface like a metal egg onto a wall of hard ice. This left the real possibility that the inmates could have gotten to the crash site and equipped themselves with the latest in military armaments, and that was not a comforting thought. However, there was a contingency plan which would make this whole strategy far simpler.

Back when the SENTRY satellite system was originally installed, a central command base was built at one of the poles of this frozen moon. This command center was used to align their orbits and to work out the kinks while bringing the system into full operation.

Knowing that they would have to leave the base behind, they made sure it was camouflaged from the surface level just in case any of the local inmates stumbled into the area. The key was to get to this base that housed the root programming and establish a direct link to the orbiting security grid. Once there, we would punch in the codes to turn the thing off, and they'll send down the troops to pick us up. Well anyhow, that was the plan.

Doc took a break from scratching his head to raise his hand ever so timidly to get the Lieutenant's attention. He brought up a good question; just *how* were we supposed to get to the surface safely in one piece? A vision of all those soldiers on the crashed military ship flashed into my mind. They didn't die quickly as one might think, I had a good idea how badly it went for them.

After all of their onboard systems got fried, they were left without any lights, communications, or any type of working life support. I could imagine the look on their faces as they were breathing the last of their air, helplessly adrift in the dark. Those few at the helm or near a porthole window would be watching helplessly as their ship was drawn in by the moon's gravity. Except for the thinning air supply, the majority of the crew would be perfectly fine. That is, until their ship slammed onto the surface at a speed that would turn almost anything into jelly. Who knows, perhaps a few could have survived. But truthfully, I doubted it.

Charlie whipped us into shape in no time and made it apparent that the mission was on a tight timetable. Each of us tidied things up in our separate departments, and we were to prepare for our drop within the week. I tried to think of several stupid excuses to sneak into the communications division to get a chance to flirt with Rook, but I never followed through on any of them. I guess I was just too much of a chicken.

Late one evening, Sarah came knocking on the door to my apartment. Honestly, I guess I had expected this confrontation was long overdue and felt a twinge of guilt to owe her an apology for avoiding her.

"Cozy little place you have here," She commented while walking in the door, "By the way, they give us girls suites that are twice this size," Sarah grinned, and I noticed that she plopped a seat down onto my bed, rather than the open couch. I was still a bit confused about how she had got involved in this whole mess.

"Sorry about not calling you back, but I was under strict orders on this confidential project, and…" I didn't get the chance to continue as she kindly butted in.

"Oh, yes, I see. Well, I was a teeny bit upset and all, that you didn't even let me know you were still alive," She argued effectively, though I was still a little suspicious that Sarah had somehow gotten herself enlisted as a mere 'supplies officer' for a secret military project.

Undoubtedly, the others were experts in their fields, and it was actually the Lieutenants connection to my father that got me my break… but why Sarah? After lightly interrogating her, I found the answer was not all that unbelievable.

"Well Jimmy, after you disappeared from work and your condo was locked out, I was so worried about you that I inquired with every police center in the sector to make sure you hadn't been murdered, or kidnapped, or something!" Sarah wasn't very emotional, but I could tell that she was serious, "And well, I thought that was a possibility, knowing what sort of a 'danger guy' you are, ever since that little incident at the bar." Okay, well that kind of made sense. "It was your department supervisor who told me that you might be found at the Confederation office."

Ah hah! So that nosy little bastard Meyers had been eavesdropping on me after all. I poured myself a good stiff shot of synthahol and sat back in the chair, casually ignoring her patting the seat next to her on the bed as if I didn't notice. Pouring a drink for her too, would only have been an invitation I didn't want to explore.

"Okay, but the rest of us on the team are all highly

qualified in our given fields. Why would Charles enlist a non-military staff member to work on such a simple job as supplies when any of his current personnel could have taken that post?" I argued. Sarah just gave me a dull disconcerting frown, as if I had insulted her competence.

"I ...I don't know. I was just so worried; I had to find out what happened to you. When I finally tracked you down to Lt. Charles, I harassed his office until he would take my call. The next day, Mr. Meyers came over to my dept and handed me a formal request issued by the Confederation with the Lieutenant's official seal," she wiggled uncomfortably there alone on the bed, "so I guess he must have needed a top-notch supply manager to do his inventory," She grinned widely, accompanied by an age-old gesture of breathing on her nails and polishing them on her shirt.

Well, whatever Charlie's intentions were, I guess it was one of those quirks of fate I would have to deal with. I made a show that I was quite comfortable where I was sitting, so Sarah finally got up to head for the door… or so I had thought. Instead, she came around behind me and started rubbing my shoulders, well, there wasn't much I could do to complain about that. My body ached as it was, but the booze and the massage felt good. Then she hit me with a whopper.

"So what do you think of our little friend, Rook?" She asked. I wasn't a linguist, but I new a catty tone when I heard one. I just kept innocently sipping on my fix and tried to act cool.

"Well, she's is kind of pretty," I replied.

"Sure, if you're into mannequins," She huffed silently, but her tone was becoming more evident. I was about to ask her if she was jealous, but that amusing thought died abruptly when I realized the gooey subject matter we would be treading onto. The one thing I dreaded more than doctors, and my phobia for hospitals, was anything that resembled a heart to heart talk. Perhaps I just needed to mature a bit, but nothing got my foot in my mouth faster than anything along the lines of expressing mushy feelings!

I had to come up with a clever comeback, and fast. I failed horribly.

"Oh, come on. You know you're quite a catch yourself, Sarah," The boozed had slowed my wits; I gulped the moment after I said that. I had shot myself in the foot trying to brush her off with an innocent compliment.

"Oh, how sweet. You really think so Jim?" Sarah poured out tenderly. Her hands on my shoulders became evermore gentle as she rubbed out the stress of the day. She began petting my hair and getting a little more indiscreet with the reach of her hands. I can't honestly say that it felt uncomfortable; I guess I was just getting caught up in the moment. It had been several years since my girlfriend had died; I guess that whole incident had really kept me from getting close to anyone else.

Sarah was being very patient, considering my cold-shoulder attitude towards her sometimes. I didn't mean to come off that way; it was just those frigid memories of my deceased girlfriend kept eating away at the back of my mind. Sarah got me another drink and turned on some soft music... and for the life of me, I don't remember what happened the rest of that evening.

෨෬

I woke up the next morning to a personal call buzzing in on my vid-screen. I didn't know how I looked, so I took the call on audio only.

"Good morning Mr. Graham," It was Charlie's voice, "It's O' six hundred hours, please report directly to the mess hall at O' seven hundred hours, *click*," As I was listening to the dialog coming over the speaker, I noticed that my shirt and pants were off, my bedding was also fairly crumpled. Sarah was nowhere to be seen. I still had my underwear on …perhaps that was a good sign. I was still groggy from the rude awakening, so I hit the shower and grabbed my notes for the day. All the while, wondering what I would do the next time I saw Sarah.

When I finally got to the mess hall, I was surprised to see a guard at the door. He inspected my badge and went over it with a portable scanner, then stepped aside to let me in. I found the rest of the crew inside, it seemed like Charlie had reserved the whole cafeteria for this meeting. As usual, I was the last to get there, and everyone was helping themselves to breakfast as they centered around a single table. So I dropped down my files in a seat across from Sarah and helped myself to a little food at the counter. I tried to avoid eye contact, but apparently she didn't seem to mind.

"Good morning everyone, sorry for the early wake-up call but we have urgent business for the day," the Lieutenant stated bluntly, "Please help yourselves to some breakfast during this initial briefing," he motioned over to the bar. Roller immediately took that as his cue to help himself to seconds.

"You will all be launching this afternoon for the specified mission," he managed to hammer out to our stolid shock, "As mentioned in our last meeting, you will be departing on a prisoner convoy to J6. As required by each transport, you will be encapsulated for your rendezvous to the surface of Europa."

Oh boy, was he laying it on us thick and fast! We all went over our notes for the project, but I can't say I enjoyed my breakfast, even though I tried. All I could think about as I stared meekly at my plate, was that this would be my last chance in a long while to eat some real food since we would be stuck on military rations during our mission off-planet; or the very real possibility that this pitiful looking dish of scrambled eggs and toast could quite possibly be my last meal.

Put on Ice

Though the Sergeant and Roller made sure we were armed to the teeth, I hid my Stinger in one of my boots. We had to wear a tight thermal-lace suit, which were webbed with sensory gear that our stasis tubes would read while we slept. Over this, we wore some pretty grungy costumes, which were just some mix-match of clothing to help us blend in with the other convicts, should we run into any on the surface.

A few of the others in the crew and I jointly felt like we were being herded like cattle for something that we weren't exactly prepared for. However, with the promise of those bonus checks being waved under our noses by Lt. Charles, we tended not to pry too much about why we were being rushed.

We finally got our first glimpse at the prisoner transport ship an hour before launch. I had seen all of its specs on paper and was familiar with the thing inside and out. The vessel itself looked far more antique than I had expected. The plan was; the main housing unit clamps were being intentionally sabotaged so that the automated mechanics would purposely fail once we touched down on J6. These clamps could be manually uncoupled once the ship landed at its destination, but it was up to Voc to disengage the self-destruct sequence that would be initiated by the onboard computer after it landed and ascertained the cargo unit would not detach by normal means.

This was the standard safety procedure for all of the transport ships, since they didn't want to take the chance of one of their ships being commandeered for vital parts in case of a malfunction. Sure, there was no usable cockpit, but hardened criminals were a thrifty sort, and could come up with a number of uses for a transport rig.

The first thing that made me nervous was that there were only eight of us, while the transport unit held a dozen tubes. When we were on our final approach to Europa, the Sentry system would scan the vessel and make sure we were all encapsulated and thoroughly incapacitated before allowing our ship to land. If it only detected eight inmates and four empty tubes, it might think something was wrong, and would either turn our ship back or zap us right there. With the way the thing was acting lately, we didn't want to take any chances.

A few days back, Min Li had provided the answer for that little problem, by providing us with a few SAC's. This stood for Synthetic Animated Cadavers, a really creepy looking ball of flesh that was commonly used in medical experiments for testing new drugs and the like. These things put lab rats out of a job and were quite effective for producing artificial vital signs for our empty tubes.

The Sergeant, Roller, and Sarah had also been working together feverishly all morning to get our gear onboard the housing unit. One of the more major concerns was that the weight also had to be accurate for a normal load that the Sentry was expecting. We were a bit upset to hear that once our ground runner and weapons gear had all been stored aboard, that it only left us with a one week supply of rations, the rest of which had been replaced with our necessary equipment needed for the mission.

Basically, the transport vehicle itself was nothing more

than a big heavy frame with a computer housed in its forward hull. It used an old type of liquid fuel booster stored in large tanks in the rear of the ship. In its cradle sat the housing unit, which was a large plasti-steel dome that was set on the surface to be used as a shelter. It was not exactly a comfortable capacity for accommodating a dozen inmates, but then again, they had a whole planet for a prison yard.

Just minutes before take-off, we all got together for a brief rundown. We were to sneak onto the planet disguised as prisoners. Once the ship lands, Voc was to disable the self-destruct sequence. It was my job to rearrange the internal mechanics to accommodate a human pilot. The Sergeant was to use the transport vessel to scout the surface for the downed Confederation ship and zero in on the abandoned command base, while the rest of us used the ground runner to make our way to its location. Once there, Voc and Rook were to run the reboot program and send the codes to shut down the orbiting Sentry satellites. Doc and Min Li were to take environmental samples during this time and provide any medical assistance to our crew and any survivors of the recon ship if necessary. Finally, Sarge and Roller were to act as our security muscle in case we ran into any hostiles during the mission.

Sarah was supposed to have arranged all our supplies and equipment so that we could work in the most linear way possible, she would know where everything was stored. I'm sure we all secretly prayed under our breath as we were being strapped into our stasis tubes.

They were tight little coffins of plasti-glass, tilted back and set neatly in separate buffering chambers. I wasn't exactly sure how these things worked, other than that they turned you into a living Popsicle… but I was about to get a quick course on Cryo-gel 101. I certainly never wanted to suffer through anything like that ever again.

* Touchdown on Europa *

The world was still bleary when I opened my eyes, and for a while I couldn't bring anything into focus. I didn't remember having dreamt anything while I was in suspended animation, but I didn't feel as cold as when I had passed out from the freezing process. The green cryogenic gel that had filled my tube was now nothing but a flaky talc-like powder. I coughed horribly after I took my first deep breath. The door to the tube had cycled open and my limbs were unbound, but my hands and feet pained terribly from that feeling of pins and needles. I was still trying to struggle with consciousness when I noticed a blinking alarm light flashing in my face. That damn computer voice boomed back on, and seemed a hell of a lot louder than I remembered.

"T-minus six minutes and counting," Was all it said, accompanied by something that sounded like a timed beep, and then it all came back to me with a jolt. I looked around; all of the other chambers were empty except for Sarah's. She was still completely knocked out, but her pulse was showing steady on the monitor above her. I'm sure Voc had his hands full disabling the countdown, but I had to get outside to the nose of the ship to see if he needed any help.

I stumbled out of the airlock to find Roller and Voc still struggling with the outer access panel. This was a bad sign. Min was apparently helping the others with their lingering disorientation, as they were all giving the two men at the front some workroom. When the speaker from the interior of the ship wailed out; "T-minus five minutes and counting," they all began to stumble away from the ship as fast as they could.

I staggered over to the front helm to help Voc and Roller while straining to get my limbs to wake up. The panel was rusted shut, it was something we hadn't checked on before lift-off that might now cost us dearly. We needed some glyceridic oil, and fast. In my muddled mind it was hard to think straight, but I knew how these ships were put together... what could I use as a substitute? As he knelt beside Voc trying to pry the access hatch open, I noticed a huge tactical knife strapped to Roller's leg and had an idea.

"Hey Roller, let me borrow your knife." I blurted out; even my voice was still half asleep. Realizing the severity of the moment, in an instant, the big lug produced three deadly looking blades out of nowhere and held them in front of me. I chose the sturdiest looking one and clambered up over the back of the dome to the center of the gear housing behind the drone's hull, which was an extremely tight fit. This area had been fairly protected from interstellar dust during its century of use and was in far better condition. Lying belly down on the rough dome, I jiggled the back panel open with the thick tip of the knife, thoroughly destroying the old rubber insulation underneath in the process. Within the compartment I had found what I was looking for.

These old fashioned transport ships still used sealed hydraulics, and I needed the fluid housed in one of those pistons. As I was wiggling one free, a loud voice broke my concentration for a second. "T-minus four minutes and counting," this was not good. I wedged the blade behind the cylinder and wrenched as hard as I could, bending the blade in the process. For a moment I feared the blade would snap off and send its razor edge bouncing into my face, but finally, the piston broke free. I grabbed it and scrambled back to the forward panel where the two men were frantically trying every means to pry open the corroded hatch.

We had a mini welder on board, but that was stored somewhere deep within our tightly compacted supplies. The cinch was, only Sarah could point out where we could find it, but at the moment, unfortunately, she was still lying unconscious in her tube. I handed the piston to Roller; he grabbed it with a massive hand and shrugged at me in confusion. I let him know what I had in mind.

"If you can break that open somehow, pour the fluid around the seal," I directed.

Without hesitation, he took hold of the piston and pulled it apart with his bare hands. Impressed by his brute strength, I reminded myself never to arm wrestle with this fellow, lest I lose a limb. He then tore a strip off his cloak in one motion and mopped up the extra machine fluid while carefully applying it to the edges of the crusted panel. From the interior of the ship came a loud monotone voice, "T-minus three minutes and counting."

"All of you grab what you can from the ship and evacuate the area, NOW!" The order came from Sarge. "You," pointing to Roller, "grab our supplies officer from the ship and any heavy weaponry you can carry," Roller looked up for an instant, as did Voc, who was charged to keep working on the uncooperative panel. In a frenzied moment, we all seized what we could from the craft and made a run for the open plain. Sarah looked like a rag doll in Roller's arms as they jogged along. We all ran, desperately searching for cover, but found none.

Since my sight began to clear, I finally took a moment to scan the landscape. We were surrounded by flat tundra as far as the eye could see. No hills, no ice boulders, nothing to take shelter behind from the impending blast. Above us in the sky, Jupiter glimmered at us in all its fury. The sight of it was imposing, and immediately made me feel like I was under a giant's thumb. All of the features of the swirling gas giant were crystal clear. Several bands of storms, wider than the Earth's diameter, layered the enormous sphere, the sight made you feel as if the whole planet was about to fall and crush you under its weight. As I stood there in awe, I almost forgot myself until the harsh computer voice shouted out across the field, "T-minus two minutes and counting."

I looked back to see the little figure of Voc struggling in vain, knowing that the orders Sarge had given him would not allow the poor man any chance of escaping to a survivable distance when the ship finally blew. If it was any comfort to think about; without any food, supplies, or shelter, we would all most likely slowly freeze to death in the days to come. In a bleak afterthought, we would certainly envy Voc and his instant, fiery death.

That was a real possibility, and I hated myself for knowing this as my conscience weighed all the facts. Those fuel pods on the transport were still half full with a combination of solid chunks of hydrogen suspended in a medium of liquid helium. In other words, when this thing blew on this open ice field, the blast wave would likely barbecue us all as well. Doing the calculations quickly in my head, I doubted that even sprinting at top speed for the full ten minutes would even be a safe enough distance.

So I stopped in my tracks. Roller had his hands full with Sarah and something that looked like an oversized bazooka. I turned around to stare back at the ship while the soldier managed only a few steps past my position, until he came to a halt and called back to me.

"Keep running!" He shouted while panting in the thin air. I silently turned to look over my shoulder.

"There's no use, really," I shrugged at him.

The big man had a confused look on his face for a second, then the slow process of fully realizing our bleak situation could be seen washing over his posture. He shuffled over and gently laid Sarah on the ground, then promptly plopped down the silver bazooka next to me and took a seat right there in the snow. We couldn't hear the countdown from this distance, but we were still expecting the fireworks.

A shout from the Sarge came from far behind us. Min, Rook, and the Doc were also with him and had stopped to see what was holding us up. I guess they were a little surprised to see me standing there with my back to them, and Roller casually sitting down as if he were at a summer picnic. Sarge was still urging us on, but we all came to a standstill, it would be any second now.

(Kaboom! With a blinding flash and deafening roar, a great ball of fire sweeping towards us...) was what I had expected to see. The burning smell of ozone and a great melted hole in the ice, scarring this perfect landscape… but I suddenly realized after a long moment that the two-minute mark of the countdown had come and gone. I could still see the spec that was Voc at the edge of the craft, but he wasn't moving. I slowly walked back to the ship, upon every step I took, fully expecting it to transform into a white-hot flash that would vaporize me where I stood.

When I finally reached the ship, I was amazed to find Voc lying on his back with his eyes shut, the corroded panel was lying next to him. I took a quick peek into the compartment, and by god, he had actually done it! Voc's tired voice hit me from behind.

"Eleven seconds to spare... Jeeze, I need a vacation," he sighed. I just turned around to pass a grin at him, he extended a hand, and I helped him up.

"Well, consider this your winter ski trip," I patted him on the shoulder, "We were just a tad worried, but I was rooting for you all along," I lied.

"Good, you can be my cheerleader from now on," He beamed back as we watched the rest of the crew slowly stroll back towards the ship. Our little jaunt had cost us physically; the level of oxygen here was far too thin to be dashing around like that. Most of us felt like we had just run a marathon, Min helped us sit down and we passed around a canteen. Sarah was finally beginning to stir, so the medic attended to her care. Sarge seemed a little disgruntled by the fact that we had all ignored his orders to keep running, but he kept silent about that.

"Where are we?" Sarah finally got to asking, her voice was a little hoarse at first. Sarge explained that the Sentry ordered every incoming transport ship to be set down in assigned sectors in random order. This was so that they didn't cluster all of the prisoners in one spot. The second reason was that this method kept ships and their shelter domes from being hijacked before the occupants could revive from their stasis tubes.

The fact was, we played the computer's game and had managed to sneak onto the planet alive. Now, we had to head directly towards the hidden Command Center.

Rook and Voc helped break out the communications gear, while the Sarge and Roller began assembling the ground rover outside the dome. As soon as Sarah got our tools out, I started working on refitting the cockpit of the drone ship. The dim sun began to set on us, so we called it a night ...and a long night it was. Each day on this frozen world equaled three and a half earth days, so to save on our power cells we began working on assembling our gear through the dark hours.

I was thinking what a grim existence being marooned on this moon must be. The local inmates must have been reduced to savages by now. No laws, no rules, no consequences. I sure as hell wanted to get off this desolate planet as soon as possible. I couldn't sleep, and took a moment to step outside during the evening to admire the incredible view of the stars; I didn't hear Sarah come out behind me.

"Romantic, isn't it?" She offered softly.

"Yeah, nice place to visit, but I wouldn't want to live here," I wisecracked as she managed a cute giggle.

"So, if we stay out here, are you going to fall asleep on me again?" Sarah inquired as I finally got a measure of insight to that evening I had lost. I just tried to act cool as if I had known all along.

"Perhaps, but am I going to wake up in my underwear again? I might get frostbite this time," I turned to her with an accusing glare and folded my arms. It wasn't dead dark outside, the clear sky let in a lot of starlight, along with the orange reflection of Jupiter across the horizon. It made the landscape appear like something out of a dream. Sarah's response was quick as always.

"I had to tuck you into bed, so I tidied up a little bit around your place, then went back to my apartment," She gazed off, turning her back on me, "I guess that's what you wanted," She finished.

"What do you mean?" I asked, not quite getting the point. She didn't bother to turn around to face me, which kind of bothered me in a personal way.

"You didn't want me to stay with you. I guess you just don't like me that way …do you, Jim?" She charged.

Uh oh, she had laid it on me, and here I was stuck in the spotlight. I guess I was a fool to hope that maybe a meteor would hit at that moment, or that a scream in the dark would break the silence, *anything* as a forgiving excuse to wiggle me out of having to answer this female trick-question. But no such luck, I'm afraid.

"Um, Sarah, I…" I never got to finish.

"You only like me as a friend, period, the end. You don't have to say it," She blurted out with a hurt tone. Being the idiot I was, I just stood there like a bump on a log. Sarah stamped back to the doorway of the shelter and cycled the panel closed behind her. As a cold wind began to sting my face, my muddled mind started to understand what she was trying to say between the lines, and I was beginning to feel like an ass.

I waited out in the howling wind for a while, waiting till I thought Sarah was asleep. I found there was no need to be such a chicken though; she didn't seem to want to look at, let alone, talk to me for the rest of the evening.

When the sun finally came out again, I had finished gutting the cockpit and rewiring the feeds to a set of manual controls. I installed the extra oxygen tholus we had stored with our gear, but I still had yet to test the hull pressure in the cockpit itself. Sarge was in a hurry, so I quickly instructed him how he could access the mishmash of the controls I had thoroughly bastardized.

Since we didn't have the convenience of a global positioning system, Rook and Voc had designed a way for us to use our radio to pick up the signal beacon from the command bunker. With Sarge in the air and the rest of us coasting along the ground, we could effectively triangulate the position of the base. In his gear, the Sarge had a special tracking unit that picked up faint signals from the black box of the recon vessel. Apparently, this was the only piece of equipment that survived both the Sentry and the crash, since all the other assigned radio frequencies were silent.

After packing all of our gear onboard the rover, we started off towards the signal beacon. Our dome had been uncoupled, and I was pleased to see that all of the controls I had wired together were functioning correctly as the transport took off behind us. Sarge would scout the recon ship from the air to see if there were any signs of survivors, and we could begin triangulating our target area. We would then rendezvous with Sarge when we reached the base. Sarah had made sure we had packed a subsurface scanner so that we could actually find the buried bunker once we were in close enough range.

Our rover hummed along at a decent click. Yet even in the day, the weather was quite frigid since our vehicle was not enclosed, built much like an open back jeep. Farther along our route, we came across a spread of jagged glacial hills that broke the monotonous landscape. The rover was built tough and was specifically designed for this type of terrain. The only difference that we had not predicted was that during the cold of night, the ambient temperature dropped drastically, and the surface snow solidified as it froze over. However, during the daylight hours, this same snow-like substance curiously reverted into something like crystallized sand.

Our buggy had thick wheels and a wide central ski, but it soon became obvious that the rover could travel faster and use less power at night when the surface was frozen. This made the Doc get all excited about his crystalline theories and such, and he took test samples whenever we stopped. During the day, Europa was like a bleached white Sahara desert but was similar to the Antarctic during nightfall. There was not much we could do about it though, as our rover was not equipped with adequate floodlights for high-speed driving, so we had to do most of our travel during daylight hours.

Praising Sarah's foresight, she had packed us sets of heavily-tinted solar goggles. During the day, the surface was utterly blinding without them, and I began to wonder if they had issued eye protection for the inmates they had sent here. Certainly, they would eventually go snow blind without some sort of protection from this glare.

We must have covered several hundred kilometers, but it was hard to say. Our onboard radio was set to the transponder, so we had no way of calling Sarge if his radio wasn't also tuned in. Rook plotted our coordinates and we headed towards the bunker. She mentioned that the transport was still moving away from us, so Sarge must've still been looking for the destroyed starship. Apparently, he was too far out of radio range to call.

It wasn't until nightfall when we started to become a bit worried. We had all hoped to reach the bunker long before now and had managed to cover a lot of ground, but a few of the others had begun to doubt that the insulated tents we had packed along would efficiently protect us from this frigid weather during the long nights.

The signal from the transport Sarge was flying had

become even weaker, which meant that he still had not turned back in our direction. This little problem hampered our ability to get our target coordinates exact, so we affixed a ground sensor to our buggy and began to zigzag over the area along our course. When the sun fully set, our hopes began to fade along with it.

Roller slowed the rover down as we desperately searched the horizon. We still had the dim light of Jupiter's glow, but there were breaks and cracks in the ice that could be missed while traveling at such speeds, which could be fatal if we came upon an unseen crevice.

Finally, a blip picked up on the radio and the Doc called out that he could see the transport in the distance. Its boosters glowed against the still horizon, growing steadily till it finally shot past us with a loud roar. Sarge pulled the ship around to do a flyby and then landed the craft far ahead. At first, we had expected him to settle the ship near our rover, so we switched over to the radio. Roller grabbed the mike as we drove on towards the ship.

"Air support 1, this is Rover 2, come in," he repeated twice more before the signal was returned.

"I copy your signal Rover 2, make your way to my landing area, over," Sarge's voice crackled in over the speaker. Roller glanced back at Rook for a moment, then put the mike back to his mouth.

"Air support 1, why did you touch down at that location, we need to make camp immediately," he asked. Sarge's answer was short and sweet.

"You'll find out when you get here, signal out… *click*." I guess that was his way of getting back at us for ignoring his orders before, Sarge did have a talent for coming across as a tight-ass every now and then.

Due to our cautious pace, it took a while to reach the

transport ship. We found Sarge standing about a dozen meters from the ship itself, inspecting something on the ground. He was holding a floodlight and waved over to Roller, then signaled him to immediately stop the vehicle. When we all hopped out of the buggy to join him, we saw what he had been looking at.

It was an enormous basin holding a concave dish, surrounded by a ring of dim yellow lights. We had found the bunker our receiver had been homing in on. Sarah however, was surprised that our sensor device on the buggy had not gone off. She headed back to the rover to inspect the unit to see if it was working properly.

"During my approach, I noticed this ring of lights. I would imagine it could only be seen from the air," The Sarge offered. He was right; we hadn't seen a thing until we were directly on top of the target area. This looked like some sort of communication dish, though without a central collection antenna. Perhaps this was our weak beacon, only a few sparse solar panels lining the dish were left clear of the encroaching ice.

Sarah unhooked the sensor from the vehicle and brought it over to the array, it only started to go off when she was within a stone's throw of the pit. Apparently, they had buried this thing much deeper than we had first thought and our schematics of the facility were wrong; or, as Doc pointed out, a century of living ice had encased the facility beyond its original design. Another decade from now it might be forever hidden under a thick frozen layer of snow.

The sensor, however, did come in handy as it located the thick top hatch we were looking for. All the men began digging until we hit the porthole with a loud '*clang*'. The snow was beginning to solidify again as darkness fell and we were really beginning to feel the cold biting at our skin. Voc used his expertise to bypass the locking mechanism and got the hatch to cycle open. We were worried for a long moment that it had somehow corroded shut and we would be stuck out here in the cold, but the metal door finally groaned and folded open as slow as a snail.

The chute below was pitch-dark. We attached our wrist and belt lights and made our way down the ladder. It emptied into a rather small chamber, and it seemed as though it was even colder down here. The large metal portal that blocked our way at the end of the alcove had no electronic locking mechanism that we could find, figuring it was designed that way on purpose. Sarge and Roller set about to cutting it open with our mini welder while the rest of us assembled our portable heaters and set up camp in the cramped antechamber to get some well deserved sleep. Sarah was still giving me the cold shoulder routine as she handed out our rations for the night. I tried not to let that bother me too much as I ate my bland meal.

I crawled into my thermal bag and nodded off while being entranced by the display of white-hot sparks showering from the electric torch Roller was using on the chamber door, all the while wondering how soon we could get out of this mess and back home to Earth. As exhausted as we were, the rest of the crew fell asleep as well. Roller finished sometime during the night, I never did hear the thick metal plate hit the floor.

When we finally awoke, it was still dark outside. Sarge went over the mapped plans of the complex again, pointing out where we would be assigned from here. Both of our doctors were ordered to complete what tests they could for the moment and to take physical readings from each member of the crew. They wouldn't have much time, since once we disengaged the Sentry, a Confederation cruiser would send down a ship to pick us up. Meanwhile, Rook and Voc set out to find the control room to the central computer and reboot the system core so they could get the shutdown sequence for the satellites and start the program running.

The Command post was designed like a maze, which was typical military thinking even for a century ago. Sarge and the technical crew set out for the central terminal to bring the power back online and get the computer up and running so they could siphon out the information they needed. We had a few portable energy cells we had been carting along just for this reason. I tagged along for the sake of curiosity.

Roller made his way to the power unit to attach these cells, which would only give us about a four-hour window to get our work done. The dim glow of lights came on in the command room as we cycled the rest of the security locks open. Both Voc and Rook went straight to work on the computer system. We had to pull in one of our portable heaters as we didn't want to drain any excess power by turning on the facility's main life support to crank up the temperature for our comfort. Still, working with numb fingers was a bit difficult.

Once he saw that our two technicians had gotten around to scanning the root programs, Sarge took off down the central hall. I was feeling a little snubbed by Sarah at the time, so I didn't want to go back to the entrance where she was neatly stacking our equipment and keeping everything in order. The two doctors were topside, taking ice and bacteria samples with their analyzing gear.

I really didn't want to get into anyone's way, so I took a little stroll about the complex. Since all the doors had been cycled open, my curiosity bug took a bite. There were stripes of different colors painted down the halls, each shade taking a different turn. As I traced these guidelines, I also noticed the doors used an old type of card swipe for access ...how quaint. Most of the salvageable equipment had been removed, which gave the whole complex a kind of forsaken aura which was not too comforting.

Only the emergency lights had come back on, and these were quite dim but efficient enough to navigate the halls, so I only used my flashlight as I searched the individual rooms. As I made my way silently down the main corridor, I noticed Sarge cross the hall far ahead of me. He was carrying a large bag, the one he had insisted on taking with him in the transport. I didn't know what he had in it, but it would be interesting to find out where he was going.

I heard the echo of his boots suddenly die, and the shutting of a portal door. When I made my way to where he had gone, I thought I had lost him. I found one of the doors shut, but without a keycard, I had no way to open it from the outside. So I shrugged my shoulders and started exploring some of the empty halls as I made my way back towards our encampment. Sarah was there going through our supplies list, she only glimpsed at me without interest as I walked in.

"Uh... need any help?" I asked, feeling like an idiot, but still willing to make amends for, um ...for *whatever* it was I did wrong to piss her off. She didn't even bother to turn around.

"Nope, I'm just about finished here," Sarah replied, but

I still couldn't read anything from the tone of her voice. Not feeling so popular with my current company, I made my way back up to the surface to see how our scientists had been coming along on his experiments. Doc and Min were busy with various gadgets and small glass cylinders filled with biological samples. When they noticed me, I broke their concentration on a topic they had been feverishly debating between them.

"Oh Jim, If I could use you a moment," The Doc asked. He closed up his instruments and made his way back towards the entrance.

"Sure, what'cha need?" I replied with a shrug.

Min Li tidied up his personal gear and followed Doc towards the chute, motioning for me to follow.

"We just need to take a blood sample if you won't mind," he asked, which of course, I did. Figuring I had to be a team player on this one, I hopped back down the chute with two scientists as they squabbled with each other about which specimen samples to take.

I fidgeted as I sat there while Sarah watched with a smirk as Min took a small instrument and held it against my forearm. It did not puncture, as he had promised it wouldn't, but it almost felt like it was burning my skin at the place where he had placed it. It also had a weird effect as I could feel my blood pulsating from the inside of my arm, which immediately made me feel queasy. After that was over, they did the same test on Sarah. She on the other hand, took it like a *real* man.

When I had asked if they had seen the Sarge up topside, they mentioned that he had dropped by to check up on their status and promptly grabbed something out of the ship. This made me curious. What did he have in that bag that he didn't want anyone else to see?

From the results he was reading, Doc became agitated and started scratching his head again. Test results from the live samples were promising and confirmed the original data from the old core sample he had studied. Even though the blood tests that Min had taken from the crew were all negative, Doc stoutly argued that was because we were still using our own water supply from our stored provisions instead of using the native surface ice, so that any results would still be inconclusive.

For the first time, Sarah seemed to be interested in the whole conversation and came over to join us. We chatted awhile until Roller came in to warm his hands by the heater. He commented on the progress our two techs were making in the computer room.

"They have been slaving over the system to find the data they need for the past two hours straight, but still nothing yet," Roller confirmed.

"But I would imagine those old systems should be a breeze to access," Doc responded.

"They should be," Roller answered with an upset tone, "but those antique computers only used hard drives, which are as slow as hell to hack."

I began to understand why the big lug was slightly troubled. If we didn't manage to shut down the Sentry system within the next few hours, there would be no Confederation rescue ship arriving to get us off this ice ball, and this bleak frozen planet would be our new home for a while.

Sabotage

Sarge wouldn't stop pacing as the clock was running out on us. We all went to the control room to see what we could do to help, but Rook and Voc were actually the only two crewmembers qualified to do the technical work and managed to drag out the information from the database and reroute it to the orbiting satellites. Twenty minutes before the plasma cells were estimated to die, Voc found a line of code that would initiate a backdoor shutdown sequence. He transferred this to Rook, who aligned the top dish to transmit the data, while we all stood back and held our breath.

"I've captured Sentry 2," Rook stated, "sending data." A white curtain of hair fell over her face as she looked down to study the console. The screen showed that the orbital was receiving, as it went through a series of reconfirmations. However, the system didn't confirm a power-down. Rook started adjusting the controls below her screen while appearing confused about what had just occurred.

"I don't understand, we bypassed the lock-out code and it confirmed it had received the shutdown data," she stated with a tone of agitation.

"Realign the dish and capture the next orbital, we'll try again," Voc cut in, and he helped her enter the new coordinates. A red light began to blink on the console that had been silent before, I took it as a bad sign.

"The dish won't realign, the motors are stuck," Rook responded.

"Or caught in the ice," Voc debated, "Try to send again

by broadband," Without hesitation, Rook attempted to capture Sentry 3, then resend. The scope on the screen showed that the wave of transfer should have been well within its range, but Sentry 3 did not return a locked conformation. Rook looked flustered as her pale cheeks turned a warm red. Doc just stood back against the wall and scratched his head. Time was running out on us fast.

Voc ripped open a panel under the console, looking to see if there was some loose wire or burnt out piece of the system that would offer him some logical reason as to why the system wasn't working. As he was jimmying something under the cabinet, one of the smaller screens came on. One word glowed into view... it read, "WHY."

"What the hell," Voc hesitated for a moment, "...*why* what?"

Rook moved over to his console and looked at the digital display, then she typed something in. The screen changed, but this time a whole sentence appeared.
    <CNTRI:4-JE6 IS FULLY OPERATIONAL AND DOES NOT DETECT ANY MALFUNCTION>.

Rook seemed a little nettled by this as she typed something else in. The rest of us were left a bit boggled about what exactly was going on. Immediately after Rook finished typing, a response appeared on the black & white screen.
    <ENTERED SHUTDOWN SEQUENCE HAS BEEN INTERRUPTED AND WILL NOT COMMENCE AS ORDERED UNTIL A PROPER DETERMINANT IS PRESENTED>.

"Oh my God, this belligerent thing is cogitating!" Voc blurted out with a gasp. Rook looked over her shoulder at him as she backed away from the console.

"What now?" She asked coolly. Good damn question.

Sarge came up between them and asked what this meant. Voc gave us all an answer that we would rather not have heard, and Sarge… well, Sarge looked as if he was going to piss himself. Voc disassembled the housing to the small screen as he explained what had taken place. He was inspecting the wires to a small frame that he placed upon the console while he was working.

The 'CNTRI' or Sentry as it was called, was installed with an AI; a very generic artificial intelligence, but one that had been revolutionary in its time. Of course, over the past century, a lot of the bugs in these systems had been worked out, since it was discovered that many of them had a one-track mind to whatever task they were programmed to perform. These Sentry satellites were originally fitted with a vast amount of memory so that upgrades could be sent by digital transmission to keep the unit current, but then, one also had to factor in the illicit data that was sent to its neural net over the years by all the corrupt Confederate Generals who were covering their own sorry asses during their reign. Who knew what warped programs they had zapped into its memory core, which was currently a very dangerous hulk of machinery with a dime store artificial brain.

All this while the machine was eating away our precious minutes of power while it protested. All three of them were sweating over the console, trying to come up with some logical reason the AI would accept to complete the shutdown sequence so we could all get off this godforsaken ball of ice. Rook typed furiously at the keyboard, complaining we could be working faster if this damn thing had voice recognition installed. But of course, this was century-old technology. Line after line, the same stagnant words flashed across the screen.

Michel Savage

<UNACCEPTABLE DATA, CLEARANCE DENIED>.

As the power started to flicker Voc slammed his fist on the console, while Rook gave a verbal blare of disgust when the whole console suddenly went dark. Each of us switched on our wrist lights and looked at Sarge for direction, but all he could do was stand there repeating to himself in a very low whisper that we could hardly make out; "God damn, God damn…"

Roller suggested that we could use the extra cells from the Rover to power the unit back up, but Voc admitted in so much technical jargon that there just wasn't enough juice in the fist-sized cells to come close to powering up this entire system. Voc disassembled the small screen from the console and placed it in his tool bag, while the rest of us moped our way back to the encampment. Sarge, who was looking a trifle distracted, told us he would catch up with us in a few minutes.

If we could only manage to find another source of power we could continue working on the data transmission with the orbital, but the old command center had run mostly on concentrated solar power, and from what we knew from the logs, those had been disassembled long ago. Well, it looked as if that pitiful little plate of eggs and toast had been my last real meal after all.

We tried debating among ourselves about what alternatives we could take, until our conversation died as we all realized the uselessness of each topic that began with the phrase 'what if'. While we were waiting for Sarge, Rook made another scan of the structural plans and found the communications room, so she headed down there to find any extra radio equipment we might be able to use.

We knew Sarge was responsible for the stellar communicator so he could call in our mayday, so we began packing our gear and setting it topside. Rook, on the other hand, had a little surprise in store for herself.

When we had first arrived, Voc and Rook had been ordered directly to the computer room to work on the data transfer, so Rook never had time to investigate the main communications bridge of the complex. As she made her way down the dark halls on the opposite side of the compound, she was surprised to see light pouring out of one of the doorways. Rook silently switched off her own wrist-light and quietly approached the door, slightly suspicious as she could hear a faint voice echoing down the hall. She was surprised to hear his voice, as Sarge was *supposed* to be over in the command room.

She snuck up in the darkness to the shaft of hard light that cut out into the frosted hallway. Since the main power was off, Sarge had no way to close the door. Apparently the extra light was coming from a portable device he had brought in. As Rook was eavesdropping, she could hear his side of a personal conversation Sarge was having with a mysterious contact.

"Negative. Plan Alpha was not aborted, it failed due to unseen problems with the Sentry's AI. Plan Beta is my only option at this time, over," Sarge was obviously making an effort to talk quietly, but Rook was still wondering why he didn't just bring the communications equipment topside for a better transmission? She continued to listen in.

"Yes… it's possible that this malfunction could be used to our advantage, and the test results on the ice were all positive. Negative, no one suspects, I have kept it concealed," his statement was followed by a long pause as he listened to the reply, "Roger, I will power up the cell and plant the egg after we break contact, and I will meet you at the Ganymede coordinates 607.1, over."

Egg? Ganymede? What the hell was Sarge planning to do, abandon us? Several wild thoughts shot through her head. Rook shimmied down to an empty doorway and hid there when she heard Sarge end the transmission and switch on his body-worn utility lights. The piercing illumination of his room suddenly snuffed out and he took off down the hall, just passing Rook as her ghostly white form backed away into the shadows. With all stealth, she followed him several paces behind as he headed directly towards the command center.

Through the shadowed doorway, she watched him set down his bag and take out a large metal canister. She had to admit that it did resemble an oversized egg. When he turned the top, it gave a slight hum and lit up around its rim as bright blue light poured out of the room. He then connected a metal coil to the console jack directly from the strange object. Rook was slightly caught by surprise as the computer powered up, and all the hall lights flipped back on. She quickly ducked back around the corner, wondering if she had been seen, but the Sergeant had his back to her for the moment.

She couldn't understand what that device was. Why hadn't Sarge helped us by using it before when their power cells went dry? She was just about to confront him when Sarge gently adjusted the rings about the cylinder, and the whole unit began to reverberate. Its low pitched whine continued to rise ever so slightly along with the glow of the hallway lights; this startled her into having second thoughts.

Rook turned around and ran down the hall to get the

others. Unfortunately for Rook, the Sergeant heard her and whipped his head around the corner. Sarge was a fit military man, and Rook never saw it coming when he tackled her to the floor. She let out a series of screams, but he quickly clamped a firm hand over her mouth and shoved a phase pistol to her head.

"Quiet there, lassie; now what were you doing running off like that. Overhear a bit of classified intel, did you now?" He whispered roughly in her ear as she tried to squirm, and he squeezed his arm tighter around her neck to keep her from struggling further. He pulled her up roughly, still holding her in a lock.

"Now I would hate to scramble the brains in that pretty little head of yours, so don't bother yelling again or I might have to pull the trigger," he threatened.

"You're going to maroon us here, aren't you," She shot back at him with a cold glare in her eyes. Sarge tilted his head with an amused look and decided to entertain her question.

"That's the plan, sweetheart. My little space taxi is waiting outside... and sorry, but there's only room for one," he spat as he pushed her forward.

Now I have to admit that I was dying to get a chance to flirt with Rook, just to see what kind of mood I might pick up from her. I didn't dare do this in front of Sarah, lest she have some sort of spiteful reaction and make a scene in front of everyone. But I was a single man, and Rook was certainly a fine example of a woman, and the frosty white skin of hers added to her exotic appeal.

When I noticed that she had taken off alone to the communications room, I figured it would be a good time to see where I stood. Sure, we had more important matters to attend to, but for the moment, it looked like we would be stuck here for a while, so enjoying the company of an attractive girl is what most would consider merely being human.

I had only bothered to glance at the digital map of the command center before I went below, and ended up getting a bit lost. When I hit the room that I thought Sarge had locked behind himself a few hours before, I found the door wide open and came across all the radio gear lying there, but no Rook. As I made my way back down the corridor, the lights had somehow come back on and I heard a scuffle in the distance accompanied by a few muffled screams. Now I'm not really the hero type, but just try to tell my subconscious that.

I sprinted down the corridor and saw Sarge holding a gun to Rook's head as they passed around a corner. Not really knowing what to think, I pulled out the Stinger from my boot and crept up cautiously.

My Stinger was a small bladed weapon, but its attractiveness was the 10 million-volt shock that it could deliver whenever it struck something. I was no weekend warrior, but Rook looked like she was in serious trouble, so I let my subconscious make all the reckless decisions for the moment. I crept up from behind, intending to just cut his arm that was holding the gun, and hoping that the shock of the Stinger would not cause him to pull the trigger. Unfortunately, Sarge was a lot quicker than he looked.

At the last second, he saw me coming from behind and turned his hand with the gun to block me. It would have worked against an ordinary knife, but a crackle of sparks flew as the pistol had knocked the blade out of my hand. The gun fired as Sarge gave a quick yelp of pain, which confessed that he was surprised at getting zapped by my knife. The sonic wave from the pulse gun missed and hit the wall above me, slightly warping the surface. The gun flew also, and I dived for it as Rook grabbed his arm to keep Sarge from getting to it first. Rook threw such a solid back-fist into the Sarge's face that it would remind me to think twice about ever pissing her off in the future.

The officer was stunned for the vital moment it took me to grab the phase gun and aim it at him. I couldn't tell what the setting on the thing was but I knew they did nasty things to living tissue, kind of like putting your cells in a blender. Rook and I backed away as he leaned up against the opposite wall, wiping the blood from his lips. Rook was rubbing her bruised hand as I was trying to hold the gun steady. I guess my nervousness showed.

"Don't move Sarge! Now what's this all about?" I blurted towards him while tightening my grip on the gun.

He looked a bit calmer than I would have expected him to, had our roles been reversed. Rook took a stand behind me as the Sergeant was recovering from her blow, wiping a smear of blood from his nose.

"He was going to abandon us here and depart for Ganymede," Rook quickly answered, "He also attached a power cell, or *something,* to the mainframe computer."

I just glanced back at Rook, and back over to Sarge whose sarcastic grin was starting to fade as the lights grew steadily brighter. I could just make out a faint hum coming from the direction of the control room.

"So, why did you pull a gun on her?" I asked a bit dismayed, also noticing the lights growing brighter by the second.

"It's not a power cell," Sarge finally answered.

"Then why don't you tell us what's going on?" I demanded.

"Come on now, Jim," he replied in a condescending tone, "why do you think the Confederation would hire a bunch of civilians to do this job?" It was a good question I didn't have an answer for at the moment.

"So why are you and Roller…?" I tried to add, but he cut me off.

"Roller is just a grunt we found, like the rest of you, I came along to personally see that the job was done. Now tell you what Jimmy-boy, if we don't get out of this compound in the next few minutes we might all get cooked," Sarge replied as he made a quick gesture towards the control room.

"You mean that was a bomb you planted… but why?" Rook relayed; not quite hysterically, but hinting on it.

"It's not really a bomb, but it will have the same effect as one. Folders are a bit unpredictable, so I suggest that we get out of here shortly," Sarge commented.

I had heard about those when I first started studying at the Academy. Electron Folders were first introduced as a universal replacement for plasma cells several years ago, but they had an inherent problem that caused them to be unfavorable for use in any type of vehicle or power system. If set incorrectly, which was an easy thing to do with these temperamental mechanisms, the protons it created would cascade upon themselves until they reached critical mass. This fault made them quite unreliable if left unattended; as what was happening at the moment, the power was increasing two-fold upon two-fold, etc. They sure made a nice little sabotage weapon.

"But why would you want to destroy the computer at this facility? It has been kept hidden for the past century, no one will find it," I asked, truly confounded by his motives.

"Oh, you just don't get it Jimmy-boy. When that thing blows, the pulse from the Folder will send a burst of feedback directly to the Sentry, thereby overloading its neural net and burn it out completely."

Okay, well that makes a bit of sense, but why did the Sarge not warn us... unless he planned on ditching us here all along. I didn't think Charlie would condone that.

"Lieutenant Charles would not authorize us to be left here while you evacuated to safety. When he finds out about this you will be court-martialed!" I threatened. His reaction wasn't what I had expected.

"Hah, ha, you think he's a Lieutenant? Charles is a Brigadier General, little man!" He responded with a practiced chuckle.

Oh crap... so all this time Charlie had been crying over the atrocities by all the cronies in the upper framework of the military, he had duped me into thinking he was one of the few ethical officers stuck in the system, when in reality, he was in on the scam.

Now I understood. We 'civilian' crewmembers were nobodies! Just a few expendable bodies who had the available skills to pull this mission off, and he got us at a cheap price. Charlie had promised each of us a load of credits he never planned on delivering, by easily turning his head and leaving us here to rot. That's why he had brought Sarah on board, because she was asking too many questions and he was just tidying up after himself.

Just then, Sarah came in tromping around the corner, muttering something about having the supplies all topside when the Sarge grabbed her before I could react. I had no idea what the range or spread of a pulse gun was, so I chose not to take a shot at him. Sarah gasped as he grabbed her around the waist and pulled out a small tactical knife from somewhere, and placed it at her throat. I wasn't about to let him have the gun back, which I think he could see in my eyes, so he slowly began backing away towards the exit. Sarah didn't struggle the way Rook had, which was a good thing considering the placement of his blade.

Around us, the lights started to get so bright they were almost blinding. A few lights down the hall began to pop, and the pulsating hum from the control room grew ever louder. I guess that was Sarge's cue to say something to resolve our waning standoff.

"Here's the deal lad, I get topside, and she lives. Don't try to follow me or make any sudden moves... I might slip," he motioned with a wiggle of his knife at Sarah's neck. So Sarge was going to desert us here on this moon, but just then something clicked into my head that made me lower the gun.

"Fine, just don't hurt her," I stated flatly.

Rook glanced at me for a frozen instant, but realized that there really was nothing we could do. Sarge dragged Sarah back through the exit and disappeared. Rook grabbed my shoulder as we waited a few moments till we were sure he was topside. When we reached the antechamber to the chute, I found Sarah sitting on the floor crying. Rook went to her, but she was fine, just a little rattled from being assaulted and held hostage.

The roar coming down the chute told me that he had ignited the boosters. Rook yelled at me to go up top and shoot him down, but I mentioned coolly that there was no need. I knew Sarge was in for a little unpleasant surprise of his own.

When we heard the ship's booster's power up, we made

for the ladder. Once topside, we saw Roller, Min, and Brendan all standing there, silhouetted against the glare of the engines as the ship took off. They all looked quite dumbfounded. Rook tried to grab a rifle from the buggy, but I stopped her as the ship was now far beyond range. It was the first time I had ever seen the look of defeat in her eyes as they reflected the dim flare of the escaping ship. I would not forget that moment for a long time.

"Everyone, we have to get out of here now!" I screamed over the fading roar of the transport. The other men just looked at me in dismay.

"Where is Sarge going in such a hurry?" Doc inquired.

"Long story, but right now, we really have to get out of ground zero!" In the darkness, the small lights that encircled the dish started to glow a searing yellow as they began to burst at random. A shaft of bright light also rose out of the chute, and the others took heed that something was definitely wrong with this situation.

We all clamored aboard the rover and Roller kicked it into gear. Its little electric motor scurried us away, but unfortunately, not quickly enough. The ice around us gave off a sudden radiant burst of light, a millisecond later it cracked and shattered, dislodging the tires and toppling our vehicle over. We hadn't strapped in, so we all went flying.

As I spun around in midair, I saw a silent scream of blue energy shoot up from the dish into the star-filled darkness above... the deadly burst of feedback from the electron folder.

We all huddled there helplessly within the chaos of falling ice and debris, with not much choice except to cover our heads and pray that we didn't get crushed. After a few depleted moments passed with us being pelted by chunks of ice, the flurry of snow began to settle. Min immediately got up and checked to make sure everyone was okay. Roller had a badly bruised arm from being thrown out of the vehicle, but everyone else was fine, just rather shaken.

The fine particles of snow were falling around us like ash as we made our way back over to the edge of the crater. There really was no reason to do so, except for the inherent human instinct to gawk at the destruction and be glad you weren't a part of it.

Well, this mission sure went to hell in a handbasket. The transport ship was now just a speck of light burning in the distance. I tried to keep track of it, but was starting to lose it among the stars. I only smiled to myself. Sarge had been in far too much of a hurry, for I had been waiting until daylight arrived to fix that broken seal near the rear housing where I had pulled out that hydraulic piston during our little emergency after we had landed.

He must have forgotten that I never completed a pressure test on the cockpit before he took off for his scouting mission the day before. I knew that as soon as his ship left the thin atmosphere of this moon, the hull would begin hemorrhaging oxygen. He would suffocate in space. Even with the extra tanks I had installed, I knew that at its rate of depletion, Sarge would not have the slightest chance of reaching Ganymede alive.

Bad News

An achingly slow sunrise spread across the horizon, lighting the scene of destruction as we began to pick through the rubble of ice for any trace of our supplies. Several of the containers had been thrown clear when the Folder erupted and our vehicle was toppled. Roller found that one of the wheels had gotten misaligned, which meant that we weren't able to travel at top speed. Several items of our inventory had been left at the opening of the chute in our rushed to escape and were now either missing or half-buried under the solid chunks of ice. It was difficult to lift any of the ice boulders clear until the sun began to rise higher and the ice started to revert back to sand-like crystals.

There was really nothing left in the crater except a blackened hole that was now starting to slowly fill with the crystalline silt. When Sarge had made his hurried escape, he had only taken his pack and thoughtlessly left behind his personal supply bag that Sarah had stowed away for him. Luckily, we now had his portion of the rations, but Sarah didn't have much good news. We had touched down with only one week's worth of supplies, and 2 full days on this ice moon was equal to a week, Earth time. We were running mighty short on provisions, so we had to thin out what we had left.

After they had ransacked Sarge's pack, Dr. Brendan & Voc discussed the practical alternatives to our situation. Within the officer's supplies, they had found some rudimentary navigational gear and a rough layout of the flight path he had taken when he set out to scout for the crashed recon ship. Sarge had never gotten around to telling us if he had actually located the crash site or what he had found there, but its exact location was marked down on his digital chart. It was a wild chance, but most likely we would be able to find at least a few containers of food, that is, if they hadn't all disintegrated on impact. It was a long shot, but the only one we had at the moment given our circumstances.

The damaged rear wheel of our open-top rover made a grinding sound as we made our way across the sandy snow. While I helped to navigate, Rook climbed over the bed of our supplies piled on the rover and took a seat next to me. I saw Sarah glance over to us, but she didn't seem to get steamed about it.

"Thank you for what you did back there," Rook mentioned casually, but I could tell the feeling was sincere. When I looked into her eyes my mood changed though, there was just something about her that made the rest of the world cease to exist for a moment; then I shook myself back into reality.

"Ah, you would have done the same. Sarge had his quirks, but he sure as hell threw us all for a loop," I smirked. Rook continued to look at the map over my shoulder as I tried to estimate the distance we had yet to travel, her closeness was a bit distracting though.

"Were you and Sarah ever intimate?" She asked innocently, that question just about made me drop my chart off the back of the rover.

"Um, no... we're just friends, co-workers at my last job. What makes you ask?" I edged out. She just brushed her bleach white hair out of her eyes and looked over to where Sarah was sitting, then back over to me.

"It just seemed that way... I was only wondering about

the way she looks at you."

I didn't know how to react to that. I found Rook had an acute talent for putting me in the spotlight, which was something I had always tried to avoid like the plague. She chose to stay sitting next to me on the back of the runner, which was fine by me, but like an idiot, I couldn't think of anything intelligent to say for a long while.

"So, how did Charlie fish you in?" I finally got the courage to ask. She looked at me again, but somehow her features had changed; a bit softer, not the hard porcelain exterior she usually presents.

"Oh, well, I had an interest in the J6 project for a long time. When I finished my tech and communications schooling at an Academy in New Hartford, I tried to track someone down at the Confederation office," Rook seemed a bit distant for just a millisecond, "You see, my brother was sent here…" she trailed off.

"Okay," was all I could manage to blurt out.

"He's not really a bad person," she insisted quickly, "he just got caught up in a bad crowd. I miss him terribly," her voice broke as she said that, while her words touched in a way that I hadn't experienced for many years. I remembered the anguish I felt that day I found my ex-girlfriend dead in her apartment as vividly as if it were yesterday. I put my hand in Rooks as a gesture of comfort. The way she clenched on tightly told me she had something bottled up inside her. Something I knew well… the feeling of loss.

"He was sent here nearly 8 years ago," Rook flashed a brief smile as she held back a tear, "Hah! I certainly never thought I would be joining him, though I'm sure he's probably dead by now," She moved her hand back slowly, and I noted that she took a quick peek around to see if anyone noticed, but they hadn't.

"For several years I tried to find out if they had some way to send letters, a message, anything. We were very close when we were children. I just wanted him to know I still thought about him, but I really just needed to know... I needed to know if he was still alive," she got her old posture back in a moment, "I was given the run-around till I chanced bumping into Lt. Charles in person. He did a background check on my credentials and offered me a job. I actually wasn't very fond of the Confederation or anything remotely to do with the military, but when he mentioned that it was the J6 project, I couldn't say no," Rook finished.

Wow, that was a bit more complicated than my boring little G-rated soap opera of a life, there was nothing about me that could really impress her. I was about to ask another stupid question when Roller called out for directions again, so I got back to navigating. To my surprise, Rook got up and moved over to talk to Sarah. Oh boy, I wish I could have listened in on that, but the roar of the wheels buried their conversation. After a while, it had seemed like they got along quite well despite my clear and apparent anxiety.

The sun had risen a good ways off the horizon when the Doc cried out and pointed towards the distance. He was using a rangefinder and had spotted the crash site first. Roller turned the vehicle to correct his heading towards the glimmering lump of silver in the distance. With the sun behind us, the ship winked at us like a beacon with every bump we took.

At least this was something to get excited about. That is, until we actually reached ground zero and saw the extent of the carnage. From my educated guess, the

Recon ship might have completed a few orbits as it lost altitude and crashed into the planet. A long furrow of snow had been scooped out of the landscape, and the ship was now nothing more than a broken skeleton at the end of a deep trench. I might have expected a few survivors if they had just a few more degrees of angle when they made impact upon the surface, which would have allowed the ship to skid along the ice; but I took a quick estimate that their approach had simply been far too sharp, let alone the telltale fatalistic velocity that showed all around the impact site. With no power, they had no way to upright the ship without the use of their boosters. The vessel might have withstood the crushing jolt to its belly, but unfortunately, they had come down on their port side.

A smear of broken metal was scattered about, as were bits of mechanical equipment and several human limbs. They must have crashed during the night, for the hard ice had cleaved a jagged scar down its center, more than half of the ship had disintegrated into confetti-sized shards.

Personally, I didn't possess a strong stomach to witness such devastation, for the area was strewn with body parts and wreckage. It was Doc who noticed something odd right off the bat. Min joined him and they started to inspect the corpses. The bodies had been fairly well preserved for having been lying here nearly three months, only a light frost covered most of the dead soldiers. I dared to take a closer look at what the Doc was pointing out. There was a fair amount of limbs lying about, but there was hardly any blood to be seen. I would have expected the surrounding snow to be stained a cherry red, but instead, only a soft tan discoloration had taken its place. A bit more of this flaky brown stuff also covered parts of the bodies, though it could be easily peeled away. Doc couldn't help himself from taking samples and logging them.

Min Li checked a few of the bodies that were still in one piece, but he didn't feel like performing an autopsy to determine if they died of asphyxiation while in space or from impact trauma... what did it matter anyway? Doc went on and on about the activity of the native bacteria and how it was retarding the decomposition of the bodies, and not in the way that was normal on mother Earth. The bacteria had somehow consumed all the bodily fluids but had fully retained the cell structures of their skin. This reminded me of the conversation we had back at the station before we all hopped off on this little escapade. He had mentioned the effects of the base elements and the byproduct of the bacteria, but I couldn't pretend to fully understand its method.

Voc searched through the wreckage for a way to get into the remaining section of the ship while Roller and I rummaged for supply boxes. Understandably, both of the women chose to stay back at the rover. We got lucky and found a few slightly damaged containers inside the hull that we had to torch open; many of the broken food containers were filled with the same fuzzy brown bacteria. Doc was ecstatic about this find, as somehow the bacteria itself had mutated into a type of mold.

In the rear of the ship, we found a smashed weapons locker containing several hundred pulse rifles and other assorted guns and gear. Most of these were bent beyond recognition; but in the mess I found a few that still worked, and just about jumped out of my pants when I accidentally fired one I was inspecting.

We brought the extra supplies over to our land cruiser

and packed what we could, since we had retrieved much more than our vehicle could ever possibly carry. To our disappointment, we didn't find a drop of purified water, all of the fragile liquid containers had been shattered.

To keep themselves occupied, Doc and Min took out some of their gear to perform more tests on the ice. Voc had disappeared into the interior of the craft for some time but finally came back with a large oval plate of electronics. The problem with all the technological gear having been 'zapped' by the Sentry was that we hardly ever used something as commonplace as mere paper nowadays, most forms of data are stored electronically. All the digital clipboards and information pads had been fried along with the rest of the onboard systems. The plate he was carrying was one of the electronic panels from the system's deck, and he had managed the delicate operation of removing its memory chips.

I knew a few things about electronics, but I had no idea how Voc made the chip's data accessible from his digital clipboard. All I can say is that he pretty much destroyed the board in the process, but he was able to pull up the files onto its display screen.

Our little scavenging party had gone quite well, considering we were even lucky to find part of the ship intact. The lack of fresh water was a problem though, but Doc insisted that the melted ice was safe to drink if we boiled it first. I was still a bit leery about consuming alien elements, not knowing exactly what the side effects might be; and I sure as hell didn't want our medic to start working on me if I caught some unknown bug. I would have complained, but it didn't seem like I would have any choice after I checked all our depleted water jugs.

We took a break back at the rover, sitting around in a

circle on top of our gear and using our portable heaters as an electric fireplace… I almost began wishing I had some marshmallows. We truly expected that the Confederation ships would be landing any day now to round up all the surviving prisoners and ship them off to the new Ganymede facility. Considering how we were duped into wearing these inconspicuous costumes, when the troops finally arrived we would be considered outlaws like the rest of the felons on this planet. We entertained the idea of taking a few intact uniforms from the corpses lying about, but for one; that thought did not appeal to anyone, and two; I doubt we could find anything in Roller's size, and three; if we ran into any of the local inmates, those uniforms would certainly make us marked targets.

All that considering how conniving Charles had been, I'm pretty sure he had our identities conveniently listed in the planetary data file as convicted felons, so that even if we did protest, not a soul would believe us. We were sure in a fix, so we decided to start working on a plan to hijack one of the personnel transports when they landed. That course of action ran a significant risk of us getting shot down by the military cruisers, but it was better than doing life without parole.

Voc had been searching through the data chips for about an hour until something strange caught his eye. The secured files he had hacked into contained all the mission orders for the deceased crew of the recon vessel. When he related its contents to our utter shock, we actually had to look at the screen ourselves to believe the audacity of what it said.

The late crew of the starship had *not* been on a true 'recognizance mission' after all. They had been directed to do a surface scan for human life forms, with orders to intercept and eliminate their presence. In other words, they weren't going to collect the surviving inmates and cart them off to a new facility... they were going to execute the prisoners and dispose of their remains!

Holy crap! If the media on Earth ever got wind of this information the Military would be in boiling hot water. The political repercussions would most certainly destroy the Confederation if they got caught, it seemed like the Council must have been tugging on their financial belts awfully tight to be brazen enough to try to pull off such a conspiracy. Needless to say, this put a little kink in our plans to hijack a transport ship when its crew would be bent on slaughtering us at first sight. Who knows what they planned to do with all the fresh new convicts that would be rerouted to Ganymede, just to find out that a prison facility didn't actually exist. Littered with the countless abandoned mines on Jupiter's 3rd moon; they could jettison the prisoners into an airless mass grave, and no one back on Earth would be the wiser.

Discouraged over this news, Doc went back to melting some snow to refill our empty water jugs. I decided to help him and brought up our earlier conversation about what effects the native ice might have on us when he went rigid for an odd moment. At first, I thought he had gotten sick from the alien water, but when he started scratching his head I knew he was thinking up something again.

"Crimany Jim! I had almost forgotten!" he spewed off while jumping for his pack in the heap of supplies. He rummaged through them and grabbed the navigational log we had retrieved from Sarge's pack. This, of course, got my curiosity up, not knowing what was going through that crazed head of his, so I went over to his side to see what he was plotting. What he had to say raised our hopes.

"I had almost forgot about it Jim. Do you remember when I mentioned the pioneering survey team that had touched down here well over a century ago?" This was more of a statement than a question. Doc continued, "They were the ones who had retrieved the original core sample that I had been analyzing. Now that I think about it, I remember something from one of the journals that had been locked away with the inventory list."

"Yeah, and...?" I urged him to spit it out.

"I can imagine it went pretty much unnoticed among the rest of the stacks of old paperwork, but I always go through personal logs and notes that are filed on such projects, and I remember reading notes that they had put a base down here for a short while, but eventually had to leave all of their equipment behind."

"I don't remember seeing anything like that in the files," I debated, but it was starting to dawn on me just what he was getting at.

"Of course not, these were old paper documents and were never transferred to digital files. They had an old interplanetary transmitter there powered by a solar array, so I can imagine that transmitter would still work," Doc stated excitedly. If he was right, we could possibly radio for help. Given it would be an old mining broadband channel, but it was certainly worth a try. We could attempt to radio Earth or any mining facility within range that might be able to pick up our distress call.

Hearing this, Roller came over and patted Doc on the back with a wide grin across his chiseled face, while the rest of the crew feverishly tried to help calculate the coordinates. Luckily, Sarah was carrying her trusty holopen, and we used it to convert the navigational data into a crude surface map. Doc had remembered its location from all the side notes in the archives he had reviewed, and we narrowed its possible location down to a ten-kilometer area, and it would be easy to spot if it wasn't swallowed up by the ice like the command center had been; however, that site had been purposely constructed underground to camouflage its location.

It was slightly hard to get any decent sleep with it being full daylight, but we managed to get some rest before setting off for the survey base. These 42 hour days were going to take some getting used to. I sat in the back again calling out to Roller whenever we started to stray from our route, which was an easy thing for him to do considering there were no landmarks to go by. The glaring snowfields were occasionally broken by tall hills and long rifts in the ice. We had to navigate these carefully, as they sometimes broke into deep chasms and shallow ice canyons. We also wanted to avoid the possibility of breaking any unseen ledges under us with the weight of our overloaded buggy.

The grinding of the back wheel had gotten much worse, but the sun was setting soon and we could continue on when the ice crystals solidified again during the dark hours by using the vehicle's built-in skis. We came to a stop and took a small break to stretch our feet and give Roller a chance to engage the sled rails under the carriage. After that, we could rest a few hours until the sun fully set, which would give the surface ice plenty of time to harden. Doc was scanning the distant horizon with the rangefinder when he called our attention that he had spotted something.

Roller grabbed the scope and verified his findings. It

was by chance that the sun was setting just then, for it was the curved shadow of the building that had caught his eye. It looked like one of the domes from the prison transports. Personally, I had expected to run into a few of these sooner, considering all the ground we had covered. We were still a good 50 hours travel time away from the location of the survey base, but by using the skis at night it would cut that number in half.

Roller discussed this situation with the rest of the crew about what we should do. Should we investigate the dome, or continue on our way? We had pulse weapons, while the local inmates had none, but who knows how desperate they might be for food. Then again, we might find nothing but frozen corpses, but it would be uncivilized of us not to warn them about the military's plan to slaughter the entire prison population.

We finally agreed that Roller and I would inspect the dome for any signs of life. Doc could keep an eye on us with the scope, and we could always use our short-range radios if we got into any trouble. Roller helped me go over the workings of a pulse rifle, telling me to expect some kickback the higher it was tuned, but to keep the setting low to prevent from seriously injuring anyone. After the sun had fully set, a surreal ruby afterglow from Jupiter washed over the landscape. We snuck off towards that dome under the gloom of dusk, wondering what we would find.

Raiders

Roller and I approached the thermal dome by starlight, leaving our wrist lamps off so that we could do so in utmost stealth, and we wanted as much warning as possible if this went sideways. After the sun had set, the winds began to pick up and the sandy snow began to solidify under our crunching boots. There were no lights coming from the small porthole windows of the shelter, and its antenna beacon was dark as well.

When we finally reached the perimeter of the building, we discovered all of our caution had been for nothing. The hatch door itself was missing entirely and it was dark as death within. Roller hit his flashlight and tried to punch the switch for the interior lights, but they refused to activate. Our flood lamps revealed the shelter had been completely ransacked. Panels, wiring, insulation, even the solar collector that should have powered the lights; everything that could have possibly been of use had already been stripped.

From the level of the frost on the floor and cabinets, this living unit had been abandoned for quite some time. When we radioed the rest of the party that the building was empty, I was surprised to hear Sarah come on the air and tell me to be careful. I guess Sarah had decided she was talking to me after all.

Roller and I presumed that the occupants had packed up what they could and took their chances out in this bleak wilderness, which meant that they had probably all come to a bad end. Suddenly, a blare came over the radio; it was Doc's voice.

"You two better get back here quick; we have three bogies out on the horizon," his voice came in loud over the speaker. Bogies? What the hell!

Roller took his mike as he stepped outside the doorway, "What is it Brendan, what do you see?" We waited in silence as the static came floating in, we couldn't see anything at all in the dim light.

"On a direct line of sight between us and your location; look out at your 4 o'clock. Several dark triangle-shaped objects; they appear to be approaching our position," Doc warned.

Roller and I strained to see what he was talking about, but we couldn't make anything out on the twilight of the horizon. Doc had the rangefinder and he must have had a clear view, so we made our way back to the rover in double-time. Even our slight jog didn't seem to help as the Doc screeched over the radio again, "I think you two better hurry, those objects are coming at us fast!"

"Do you see any lights?" Roller asked quickly.

"No, no lights. They look like... wait..." He trailed off. We picked up our pace and as we approached the rover; everyone was hopping aboard the vehicle as Dr. Brendan was standing on the highest crate looking at something through the scope. It still took us a few more minutes to reach them. Doc ran out to meet us and handed Roller the scope. The big soldier took a quick look in the direction Brendan was pointing; it took him a few odd seconds until he caught them in his view.

"They look like sails," He added. This sure shocked me... sails? I grabbed the scope from Roller and took a peek, as I adjusted the focus I saw what looked to be land-sails. I had seen a windjammer race when I was a child, but they were used on the salt flats out in the desert. These large sail ships seemed to be held up by blades instead of wheels.

Doc was right; they were gaining on us fast. There was a quick debate on what we should do, though our minds were pretty much made up as our bodies did the talking when we all jumped aboard the rover. Roller gunned the electric engine and we sped away, luckily he had mounted the skis before we had left to inspect the dome. The three sail sleds had several people mounted on them, perhaps four to each, but it was hard to tell.

Sarah asked why we shouldn't just maintain our position and try to befriend them, and perhaps keep them at bay with our guns if they turned out to be hostile. Both Roller and Voc answered her question in parts. First, if they were roving scavengers who had managed to construct an ingenious method of transportation across the ice, then they might have been just thrifty enough to construct some type of lethal weaponry. Secondly, they outnumbered us, and Roller didn't want to find out if they were armed or take a chance of letting them get within range.

Our rover and all the supplies we were carrying would make a pretty sweet prize. Convicted criminals couldn't help their reputation. There was a good chance they just might befriend us as a ploy to gain our trust, then slit our throats the first moment we turned our backs for all the gear, food, and weapons we carried. It just wasn't worth the risk.

Our tension began to ease when we realized they were losing ground. With the skis on, the rover was just too fast for their wind-powered sails. Still, traveling near top speed like this in the dark was exceptionally dangerous, as we might come upon a cleft in the ice without time to maneuver.

A few hours had passed and we spotted another dome in the near distance. Like the one before, all of its lights were out, and it seemed like parts of its external shell was missing. Needless to say, we didn't bother to stop. Sarah took a moment to crawl over to where I was sitting in the back with the scope, keeping an eye out to see if we lost our pursuers.

"Are they gone?" she asked while peering into the darkness. I put the range finder down.

"No sign of 'em. How's your neck?" I asked.

Sarah felt the little red line where Sarge had put the knife to her throat; it was just a superficial cut, but had healed fast.

"Okay, I guess. I can't really see it, but it doesn't hurt though," She took a look around at the stars above us. Jupiter had started to rise over the horizon, a big candied ball of orange and white expanding like a cosmic tidal wave. It really was a spectacular sight. The rising planet reflected a soft orange glow across the landscape; at least this would give Roller some light to steer by.

"Hmm, I thought you weren't talking to me?" I gave a slight chuckle as she offered an innocent shrug as a response, "Look, Sarah, you're great to be around, and I'm sorry if I did anything to... anything to hurt you," There, that wasn't so hard to say after all. I still had a lump in my throat that had appeared out of nowhere. Sarah put her arm around my shoulder and gave me a quick peck on the cheek. I guess, maybe I wasn't such a jerk after all.

After traveling over a few small hills we hit another low plain, but something caught our eye. Roller brought the vehicle to a halt at a thick dotted line that scarred the ice, and we all hopped out to investigate. It looked like it was fairly old, a few centimeters beneath the surface layer, but still very visible.

Min Li took out his med counter and analyzed the opaque markings. He reported that it was composed of some sort of synthetic petroleum substance, though its exact origin was unknown. The real question was; what was its purpose? Roller took a walk down its length a ways, till he turned around and called to the others. He ordered everyone into the rover and he turned the vehicle onto the odd track.

"What is it Roller?" Voc asked.

"Look at the line ahead," Was his only response.

We all craned over the edge of the vehicle as we passed what appeared to be an arrow drawn into the ice with the oil residue. The dotted line ran off into the horizon, and we passed a few more arrowheads that guided our way. I don't know what Roller had in mind as I tried to relate to him that we were straying from our heading to the survey base. He only cited some vague facts about his previous tactical training, although he didn't mention anything about the Confederation. I could imagine he wasn't rather fond of their ranks at this moment, just as much as the rest of us weren't.

Upon approaching a long line of hills, we began to see the soft glow upon the horizon from a source of artificial lights. The jagged stained line led straight into a hollowed pass, so we edged the vehicle to the side of the bank far off the path. Still hidden within the cool shadows, we crept up to the edge of the hill on foot. To our astonishment, we found a dimly lit village nestled at the bottom of the drift.

It was actually more of a shantytown than a village, but

considering the hostile environment, it was certainly a flag of achievement owed to human ingenuity. There were several inmates walking around, all going about their business. A half dozen wind-sails with lowered masts sat parked in the far corner, while numerous individuals were busy hauling scrap metal to certain areas. This was the first sign of life we had run into, but certainly not what we had expected to find.

Doc passed the scope between us, and we found many of the occupants engaged with duties that vaguely resembled a medieval town. One particular man walked about surrounded by several bodyguards; they were armed with makeshift swords and wore crudely constructed crimson armor made from bits of steel and thick plastic. We quietly crawled back down to the buggy and debated on what to do.

"In concern for our own safety, I do believe that we should make our way directly to the survey base and try to call for help," Voc suggested.

"Yes Voc, you're right… but in due conscience, we should at least attempt to warn these people that it's very likely we are all going to be liquidated before the next sunset," Roller added solemnly. Seems like the big lug had a lesson in ethics he chose to lay upon us.

"What good will that do, they have no way to fight back? Besides, these convicts belong here, we don't!" Sarah let in, "The best thing we can do for ourselves *and* them is to get to that base and radio for help," Her point was well taken, but Dr. Brendan brushed his way in to our moral debate.

"I would like to examine these subjects more closely if I could get the chance," Doc offered as he turned to our medic, who also nodded in agreement.

These scientists and doctor types just wanted the opportunity to pick something apart and put it under a microscope. Roller would not let up that it would be uncivilized to let these people get slaughtered without raising a finger even to warn them about the Confederation's intentions. Since we were already in garb that would let us meld into the crowd, the chances of getting caught were justifiably slim. He proposed that we confront at least one of them with our warning, and then we could leave as quickly as possible. We suggested that the women should stay behind with the buggy, but Rook would hear nothing of it. She wanted to find out if someone might know what happened to her brother, and there was little we could do to stop her. Rook could certainly take care of herself; I remembered that bloodied back-fist she had given Sarge.

We had to make some quick wardrobe adjustments, like concealing our guns and radios. Sarah volunteered to stay with the rover and guard the supplies, although I doubt she had ever fired a weapon in her life. We edged our way back over to the marked road, and slipped in one at a time on foot so as not to draw any attention, and began inspecting the town.

I recognized bits of thermal domes and other gear that had been scavenged. The artificial lighting had come from several disassembled solar arrays stripped from the guts of their thermal shelters. I was also surprised to see internal braces from starship hulls and several panels from other types of transports. Apparently, the recon vessel had not been the only spaceship to have ever crashed here over the ages.

Roller was just looking for someone to talk to, but Doc and Min were eyeing everyone with a little too much zeal. Most of the inmates seemed a bit worn, even malnourished, as a few displayed dreadfully thin waists and their stomachs were completely sunk in. It was grossly unnatural, just looking at them made me feel nauseous. Rook hid her face effectively with a scarf, and her trench coat concealed her healthy figure. There wasn't much Roller could do about his size, but the ragged coat he wore helped him to blend in with the other miscreants. I tried to act casual, but in reality, I was nervous about walking into this vipers nest.

Most of the people didn't pay much attention to us, and the deep shadows from the lamps helped conceal our faces, but there were a few who did notice us outright, and our blown cover soon became painfully obvious.

Roller stopped one fellow who had walked out of a rusted structure and spoke to him in low tones. I don't know if his advice was of help, because the little man immediately ran off. Roller turned around with a look of bewilderment as if he had only finished half a sentence when the fellow had so rudely departed. I don't know what he said, but I got this funny feeling something was wrong when I turned to notice a few people in the distant shadows pointing at us.

Out of the same decrepit structure came a ruffled-looking old man with a lazy eye and unkempt stringy white hair. He sported a ragged sweater and looked at us with interest through a pair of spectacles that had one of the lenses missing.

"You're not from around these parts, are ya?" He mentioned casually as if he saw right through our disguise. I was about to reply with some stupid remark that I was commonly famous for, but was interrupted by a shout from somewhere behind us. The man with all the bodyguards was closing in on us, and I knew our goose was cooked.

When he yelled at us to halt a second time, Roller gave us a quick motion to disperse. I think Voc got about five steps before someone grabbed him, and Min didn't fare much better. Dr. Brendan tried to duck into the shelter as the lazy-eyed man just looked on in amusement; I bolted in the opposite direction. From nowhere, I got clubbed in the gut and dropped like a stone. I must have blacked out for a second, for I didn't see how they had managed to get Roller. Rook herself, was nowhere to be seen.

We were all bound by the wrists with our arms held behind us and dragged up to our feet as the VIP approached. He gave Roller a quick sizing up with his eyes and reached inside his coat behind his back to grab the concealed gun from his belt. This caused a few murmurs from the surrounding crowd. Roller tried to struggle for a second, but the guards edged their swords into his side just enough to settle him down.

The VIP held the silver gun up to the light in admiration. "Well, well, what do we have here?" Giving a sarcastic grin back over his shoulder to Roller, "Take them to the chamber for questioning," he ordered. Roller tried to shout about something but he was quieted by another jab to the ribs as we were hauled away.

This chamber he was talking about was a large oval structure in the middle of the complex, made from the shell of a starcraft that had either been dragged there by some means or built upon where the ship had settled. It was patched together with bits and pieces of scrap and the interior showed signs of an old design. They made sure we were all tightly bound with strips of cable and we were thrown into an unlit recess. The door had been missing, only a pitiful strip of cloth hung over its entrance letting in a trace amount of light.

"Well, this certainly didn't go as planned," I muttered. Roller was about to apologize when the rest of us corrected him. It was the right thing to do, and we all had come in here knowing the risks. A guard suddenly barged in and issued Roller outside, threatening him with a jagged spear to obey promptly. We all sat there in the dim shadows as we strained to overhear the distant conversation; Roller's voice was part of it. It was several minutes till he was thrown back in with us, and we each took our turn at the interrogation. I was hoping they would take me last, and I got my wish.

They took me to what was once the helm of the ship. The captain's chair had been removed, turned, and repositioned in a more convenient place to face an audience. Within it sat the VIP who had ordered our capture. He had Rollers handgun stuck in the front of his belt, as if it were a prize on display.

"Your comrades say that you walked here, but I don't believe that's likely," he stated with confidence. His eyes were heavily browed and he bore a deep scar beside his left ear. It was obvious he had an authoritarian air about him and was not someone to jerk around with indirect answers. I just tried to give as little information as possible, figuring that my companions wouldn't dream of telling them the whole truth; like we were Confederation agents, active or not.

"Yes, we came across the lines in the snow and followed them," I blurted out slowly, hoping this fit in with whatever story the others had told him while hoping this guy was not too bright.

"The Heavy in your party tells me you guys found this

gun at a wreck, were there any more there?" He stated while patting the gun at his waist. This sure sounded like a trick question, the others might have answered yes or no, and a transparent lie would not help my situation.

"I don't know, I didn't go inside the wreckage," I blurted out, trying to act dumb.

"Let me get one thing clear to you runt; I am Turvel, get to know my name because I run this complex! While you are here, you will do as I say, or you will either be banished to the wastelands of ice, or I'll kill you myself!" He threatened with a psychotic smile.

Obviously, the guy was up for hard labor or he wouldn't have let us live if he suspected that we were anything less than fresh-meat convicts that had been recently dumped here. We got lucky, and I was glad now that we hadn't changed into those military uniforms. The guards took me back to the holding cell, but they didn't bother to untie us.

A long time passed while we waited for what might happen next. For the moment we had passed off as fellow inmates, but if they discovered our buggy outside, that would certainly get us lynched. We had to find some way out of this complex before sunrise; and I just prayed Sarah didn't try anything heroic.

The same creepy bystander with the lazy eye came into our cell room and looked us over thoroughly. This made us all a tad nervous because his movements were very erratic as if he were schizophrenic.

"The word is my friends, that you told my partner a bit of juicy information about the Confederation. That the Law is gonna come down and wipe us out?" The skinny man offered to our faces.

"And who are you?" Min asked abruptly.

"Me? Why, I'm Dr. Roy Leer; but please, call me Professor… everybody does, ha, ha," He finished with a bow and a hysterical cackle that made us raise a brow. Well, that certainly confirmed that he had a few screws loose.

The Prof stated that it was his responsibility to lay out the rules and operations for all the greenhorns that came this way. He took his time untying us and gave us the rundown on all the expectations of their boss; Turvel. Under the watchful eye of the armed guards, we followed the Prof back to his little shack while he pointed out the functions of the base along the way. Of course, we were just humoring him until we got the chance to make a clean break for it up over the hill and into our buggy, then we could leave all this madness behind us.

Though as unbalanced as the Prof might have seemed, to the Doc and Min's surprise, he was actually quite learned in several fields. When he pressed us again about the warning we had given concerning the Confederation, we decided to convince him of our integrity.

"Well now, you say they are going to come down and wipe us all out? Hah-ho-hah, I was wondering when they might pull a stunt like that; so they finally found out…" he giggled. This made us a bit curious about what he was leading onto, but Doc cornered the conversation on him.

"Found out what?" He inquired, pretty much knowing the answer already. The Prof was more than willing to entertain our feigned astonishment.

"Why, about the ice here. How it *changes* you. The politicians back on Earth would give their left leg for a hunk of this 'ole rock ice, *heh-heh*."

This was what Doc had been hoping to hear. All of his research on an old ice sample was nothing compared to actually getting a chance to poke and prod at a living patient. Too bad all his gear was back at the rover.

Thinking we were just newly transported felons, the Prof gave us a rundown of what effects to expect. Giving us all full warning that food rations were very scarce, but if you could manage to get by after the first few months, you wouldn't notice the transformation so much. The two scientists egged him on for specific details that would have annoyed any normal person, but the Prof wasn't one of those... not even close.

He mentioned that after several weeks of living here, one's diet begins to change. Apparently, he had greater knowledge about the bacteria in the ice than we would have expected. But it was also rather foolish of us to assume that everyone exiled here was a former drug lord, mass murderer, or back-alley thug. There were a few white-collar criminals that had been discarded here and the Prof was one of them. He mentioned how he had been convicted of performing outlawed research with clones, something that wasn't too popular in the political or public forums.

He once had his own private tech lab in bio-engineering and had created live specimens of former colleagues without their knowledge or consent. I could imagine it would be disturbing to find out that someone had created several test clones of you and your fellow coworkers for their own personal experimentation. Our Professor here had been found guilty of crimes against humanity and a few other misdemeanors he was more than glad to mention.

Doc and Min finally weaseled out some relevant facts

about extended exposure to this environment. The Prof stated that boiling the ice to make water was one of their accidental drawbacks, as the high heat kills the bacteria. If the ice or snow was slowly warmed until it began to thaw it produced a slush of sorts, this essence could then become the main staple of their diet. Finding areas of greater concentration of the bacteria that grew in mass veins could greatly magnify its effects.

He mentioned how most of the newcomers usually got straight away to slitting each other's throats the moment they popped out of cryo-stasis and discovered the severe shortage of rations stored in their supply bins. He mentioned how over the years the food shipments had slowed down to almost nothing, and how everyone transformed into bloodthirsty scavengers fighting for survival. What they once needed as a few meals a day dropped down to one, then maybe solid nourishment once a week or longer. He gave a descriptive analogy, comparing the metabolic changes, like snakes of Earth that could get by feeding only once a month.

Living here under the unnaturally long days and nights made it difficult to keep track of time, and many lost their sanity entirely. We could witness that from right where we stood. The Prof lifted his sweater and showed us his depleted gut, much to my disgust. He stated how he had performed many autopsies on fellow inmates, and how their intestinal tracks had shrunk. When he casually mentioned that he also had a secret lab here in an old survey complex, we all froze like statues.

"You know where this complex is?" Roller asked suspiciously, not wanting to give away his hand.

"Why of course, been using it fer years, but you ain't gonna find it; and if you tell anyone, I'll deny it. Ain't nobody will believe you either, *hmph*," he threatened with a tiny fist, realizing that Doc and Min had tricked him into blabbing a secret, but after a moment he got wise to us.

"Hey, how is it you know about that base too if you ain't ever been there? How long have you been out on the ice? I seriously doubt you fella's been wandering around the dunes on foot and just happen to make it all the way here without any supplies… and how do you know that the Law is coming here to liquidate all the inmates?" He started to get riled, "You young punks better tell me the truth, or I'll warn Turvel that you all are trying to cause trouble, and he'll fix you good!" Dr. Leer spat at us. We gave each other a quick worried glance. Either we had to tell him some elaborate lie that might get him to start yelling for the guards, or give him the facts… Doc was the one to blab first.

The Prof had a profound look of astonishment on his face, but he didn't call for the guards, which was a good thing. If he had, Roller could always snap his neck if he started to scream for help. We were all startled that he actually found our story funny. I guess you had to have a sense of humor to keep a measure of your sanity in a place like this, though the Prof was riding the razor's edge on that theory.

"Eh, well, this is certainly an interesting situation," he gleamed, "I can show you how to get to the base, though most of the rooms and equipment are locked away behind heavy steel doors. Ain't no way you're gonna open them without power either."

"We have a few plasma cells, and I can hack the access circuits," Voc added.

"Ah, well, that would certainly be a benefit, I couldn't

figure them out myself, no way to get the panels open. The whole complex is completely covered in ice. You could walk right by it and not know it's there," the Prof exclaimed while rubbing his stubble-ridden chin, the same way Doc was scratching his head. Two birds of a feather I guess, although the Prof dabbled on the unethical side of the fence.

"We have the tools, plasma torches, whatever we need," Roller put in, trying to forward his point. The Prof just looked him up and down with a sheer grin on his wrinkled face.

"So, what, you got all these things hidden in your pockets big boy, or is all your gear stored away somewhere… is there something you're forgetting to tell me, son? Your little team here must have some sort of transportation to be gett'in you around I think," the Professor finalized. Grudgingly, we had to admit we had a land rover, extra guns, and supplies. The Prof was thoroughly excited about that, especially that we were going to nark on the Confederation Council.

"Heh, I don't care if them bastards on Earth are having a food shortage, I just want to see the Council go down and put *them* fools on ice for a change."

"What do you mean Professor? The food shortages have been over for quite some time, how long have you been here?" I had to ask.

"Um, hmm, let me see, since I got sentenced here I've been keeping a Terran calendar marked on the walls or whatever I could find. I would say its been well over seven thousand days now… that's hmm, about 20 yrs ago I guess." The Prof exclaimed.

"You mean a daily calendar," Voc asked warily, "…in *Earth* days?"

The Professor gave us a confused look, "Why um, no. When they dump us here they don't give us clocks of any kind, just 7000 days on this moon, I'm guessing."

Voc looked at us all in astonishment as I slowly began to realize what it meant when I did the math in my head. The Prof had been convicted in his late 60's and dumped on Europa to pay for his crimes, but 7000 days on this moon was well over seventy years in Earth time, which made him one healthy old coot for being over 140 years old. No wonder he was going crazy, doing *life* on this rock was excessive punishment.

Dr. Leer got a wild look in his eye as if he had made a critical decision with whatever sanity he had left.

"You don't know how long I've been waiting for a break like this to get away from these thugs that run this joint, and I ain't gonna let nobody screw it up for me now, so here's your choice," The Prof lowered his voice to a menacing tone, "I won't tell anyone that you're actually Confederation agents on one condition ...you have to take me with you!"

Survey Station

After reluctantly agreeing to his demands, the Professor left the building and went to talk to a few of the guards outside who were keeping an eye on the area, and on us. Shortly thereafter, he came back in and grabbed a few knickknacks, and handed us a few empty sacks to carry. This was to make it look as if we were joining him on a little excursion to retrieve scrap metal and equipment from our old dome shelter... at least that was what he had told the guards.

We kept an eye out for Rook who had disappeared since our capture, but we shortly found her as we made our way over the rise.   Her raggedy black cloak had apparently helped her to hide in the shadows and escape our captors. The Prof was a bit shocked when he first saw her, the combination of her dark hood contrasted against her snow-white skin made her look like a specter. When Rook recognized us, she lowered the sonic rifle she was holding and stood aside where we noticed two unconscious convicts stretched out behind her, both hogtied and lying face down in the snow.

Rook had instructed Sarah to move the buggy behind a small dune a short way off, where she was waiting for us. Roller made sure that the Prof was not free to handle any guns whatsoever, which made the old man scowl but he didn't complain much about it.

The Prof examined our crude map and made a few corrections on our course by his own observations of the stars. Europa had a slightly tilted magnetic pole just like Earth, so I adjusted our heading according to his specs.

We were quickly on our way but were further warned that the prisoners on this moon had adapted to becoming nocturnal, as they had not been issued protective eyewear when dumped here, and the blinding white landscape was a natural hazard of the daylight hours. He also stressed a few facts, such as; that their sled sails could only be used when the ice hardened and the wind picked up at night.

Doc had a whole bag of questions for the Prof as we bounced along on the rover, about how the environment had changed them physically. The Prof stated that he had spent much time using the lab facilities at the survey base and performed experiments to pass the time. It all had to do about how our bodies converted the unique properties of the bacteria in some fashion, turning them into usable calories on a limited liquid diet. This was certainly one for the medical journals, and Min took a few scans at the Prof with his diagnostic gear.

Sarah handed the Prof a few rations that he devoured immediately, stating that Turvel kept tight control of all food stocks, using it in trade for labor, showing just how provisions had become the main type of currency at this penitentiary. He explained that over the years a few ships would crash here from time to time. These were usually just a few unlucky souls who had enough credits on hand to charter a ship or had stolen one in an attempt to rescue a comrade or accomplice off this planet-wide Penal Colony. Little did they know just how effective the orbiting Sentry actually was, which had now become the self-appointed warden for this accursed ice moon.

From what he had heard, no rescue attempt had ever succeeded. The Sentry would shoot any vessel down with a powerful gamma-ray burst, much like a hyper-concentrated solar flare. Several broken hulls lay spotted across the frozen landscape. These were scavenged for parts and supplies by the mercenary groups on they're sailing sleds that were known by the locals as 'Raiders'.

The Professor mentioned that he was very lucky to have lasted this long, as he had seen many petty tyrants like Turvel come and go. They were usually hunted down or murdered in their sleep for the top-dog position in this chaotic hierarchy. Chaos thrived here, as there were no laws or consequences to fear.

Doc kept an eye out with his scope and spotted a few Raider ships in the distance, but they had apparently not noticed our land buggy as Roller was guiding us along with our lights purposefully switched off. We were only traveling at half speed and didn't want to take the chance of being seen.

Voc asked about the dotted lines in the ice we had noticed before, to his satisfaction the Prof explained. The inmates didn't have the convenience of a compass, so they used excess oil and engine fluids to draw massive lines several kilometers long around certain important complexes or junctions, such as the one we were captured in. There was a straight line for the north, broken line for the south and various dotted lines for east and west. This was so that the Raiders could use them as a guide when they came across these markings. Also, the use of celestial navigation was helpful; they weren't all illiterate hoodlums you know.

A few rival groups had used downed starships as their main bases, but after a few years, these too would slowly begin to be swallowed by the ice, much like the old Command Center had been.

As we were driving along, the distant sun glared at us as Jupiter began to meld into the horizon. The Prof grabbed

Michel Savage

the scope from Doc and helped me plot our course. For the time being, we would be safe from the raiders; as the evening winds began to die with the coming of dawn.

There was a strange structure up ahead that the Prof guided us around; a huge hollow pit filled with crystallized barbs of ice. Doc had to stop and take a few moments to investigate this strange phenomenon. The Prof explained that this was just an old crater where a meteor had struck several years ago, and the area of the rim had contracted much in size since then. The Doc could not help himself but to take a few samples while wandering through the forest of icicle trees. It was truly an amazing sight to see; however, the Prof just rushed through with careless disregard, kicking a weak stem here or there out of his way as they fell to the ground in a mass of broken shards.

As the sun peaked over the horizon, the small grove lit up with a million prisms of colored rainbows, it was like something out of a fairy tale. Doc was trying to fathom why the ice would react this way. Logical science would suggest that the snow would just cover the crater with slow drifts, but the way it was reacting was almost like rock crystal, not resembling water-ice in the slightest.

After our quick tour through the shimmering ice forest, we boarded our buggy and adjusted the rovers steering skis and put it back onto its wheels. Doc tried to struggle with a theory why the crystallized ice-sand would change so dramatically by day and night, but the Prof corrected his thinking that it was solely the temperature that effected the mutation. As it turned out, it actually had something to do with the photosynthesis of trace bacteria in the ice. He stated that in the areas along the faults the transformation was even more dramatic, and promised to show him sometime when they had the chance.

It was along these fault lines that the oxygen levels were much higher, due to some sort of emissions from deep within the ice, maybe even as far down from the liquefied depths of the ocean. Living on the bleak surface, I had almost forgotten that this moon was one planet-wide frozen sea, but remembered the logs that the ice was just a thick mantle floating on a watery layer.

The Survey records Doc had reviewed mentioned the mining industry had settled a team on Europa to drill through the icecap in order to get a determination on its depths, hoping that there was a sedimentary bottom that was feasible to reach. Unfortunately, their records only stated that the layer was thicker than expected, so they abandoned the operation. We were just hoping that all the equipment they had left behind was still intact.

When we approached an odd hump in the snow, the Prof jumped up on the back of the rover and shouted that we had arrived. He had been right, we would have easily passed up this dune-like formation at any distance. Even though the base had been originally constructed above ground, it was now completely enveloped by the living ice. At the surface, we found a snow cave that the Prof had maintained over the years that led down and around the bleached plasti-cement walls of the complex to the large central bay doors below.

The naturally white structure is probably what had kept it hidden all these years, acting as a type of camouflage that helped it blend into the environment. Now that it was covered with ice, it was certain that the base would never be found by anyone who didn't know its exact location. As he led us down inside the translucent cave, the Professor informed us how he was lucky to have stumbled upon this facility when it was still only half-buried. In the middle of his story, we came upon the cracked double doors to the loading bay.

The interior of the bay was lined with several large glass and steel vessels, along with various crane equipment used for moving them within the cargo area. The Prof led us up a short stairwell to what was once an observation chamber and into his makeshift laboratory beyond. It was obvious that he had used an assortment of scraps of whatever he could find to assemble his workspace. Doc was flabbergasted by both the crassness and pure ingenuity that was the result of the semi-workable stations. It soon became clear to him that the Prof had been using long-outdated techniques to acquire the results and observations of his tests.

There were several computers in the room that Voc immediately went for; however, the Prof suggested that a few of us go up top to scoop away some of the snow to clear off the solar panels lining the roof. Roller volunteered so that we could get some power to the terminals, and headed out to the rover to get a utility shovel. Doc stayed behind to look over the lab and frequently asked the Prof about certain gizmos whose function he failed to fathom.

Sarah stayed by my side as both our technicians took a look over the terminals, while every so often Voc would let out a chuckle at the sheer queerness of the antique computers.

"By God, these old things used gigabyte hard drives to compile data," he laughed while glancing at Rook who was trying to figure out the mess of wires. Our modern military gear would allow us to analyze data cubes or information rods, but this technology was far behind from what we were prepared for back at the command center.

"Well, you might as well get comfortable," the Prof added, "even when that big guy gets the solar panels cleared it will still take several hours for the batteries to recharge."

Voc thought about just taking one of our plasma cells out of the rover for some immediate power but soon found that solution would be impossible since this system was such a dinosaur. Rook managed to figure out that the terminal she was playing with was solely for internal transmissions and was not the central communications hub that she was looking for. The Prof admitted that there were, in fact, several more chambers to the complex that he had failed to gain access to. He was not a computer expert, nor had he any idea how to hotwire the access panels.

He led Voc to one such door, which was a massive steel portal. There were no quaint keycard slots like the command center had, instead these worked on some sort of twelve button keypad. After prying away the panel, he admitted that we would have to wait until the power kicked in before he could run any diagnostics.

We went back to the lab, and Sarah lent the Prof her holopen to draw out a map on the tabletop. He was astonished by the marvel of a pen that could write with light on any surface, but Sarah made sure he handed it back when she noticed him trying to nonchalantly slip the tool into his pocket. Back when the complex was still only half-buried, the old man noted there were a total of five interconnecting domes. All of them coupled to this central main bay, mentioning he failed to find any other entrances from the exterior but admitted that they might have already been buried beyond sight.

In the section we were currently occupying, he pointed out two separate doors that led to the adjacent domes, and a third which led to another chamber. After Roller joined us from his project topside, we had all planned to get some much needed rest. After we set up the portable heaters, Doc and Min decided to stay up to hash over the Professor's findings. The trio made a tour of the mismatched tubes and other odds and ends that the Prof had assembled over the years.

Doc finally took the opportunity to explain to the Prof that the time the old man had spent on Europa was over three-fold of what he had expected. Understandably, the Prof was a little taken aback by this news, until they worked out the math for him and proved the length of the moon's cycle.

Min was anxious to do a few more skin and blood tests on the poor Professor, who grudgingly agreed in the name of science. I couldn't help but overhear their squabbling in the next room, puzzling details of genetic science and bio-engineering that shot back and forth across the lab. Unfortunately for me, my sleeping bag was placed nearest the doorway.

As I was about to nod off, I could hear them bickering with each other and offering thesis over their perspective research. What I overheard made me realize the true irony of this situation. Doc had casually mentioned that the Confederation was losing funding when a large mass of the Earths population had decided to colonize off-world, either for terraforming projects across the galaxy or working on asteroid mining facilities. The Council was now looking at the J6 project in a new light as their golden piggy bank and was planning on selling this new youth drug they could produce to all those estranged intergalactic colonies, thereby drawing them back into their financial net.

When the Prof broke out in a burst of hysterical laughter at this news, he nearly woke the rest of the crew that was bedding down in the adjacent room. Doc and Min had to take in the full story to understand his view on the situation. I could hear him tinkering with vials and shuffling through charts as he tried to explain through his erratic mumbling.

"So I understand that you haven't run into many inmates on the planet so far... but tell me what it is that you haven't seen at all here on this moon?" The old man asked his guests.

The Doc didn't know how to approach this question and took a moment to ponder over it. However, the Prof was eager to jump to the punch-line.

"I'll tell you. Now you have to realize that there are nearly as many women as male felons that are shipped off to this frozen hell, and sure, they aren't as strong of survivors as most of the thugs around here, but still, everyone has their human side... man cannot live on ice and water alone, if you know what I mean, *heh-heh*."

Doc and Min Li were beginning to contemplate what he was getting at, but still struggled to grasp exactly what he meant. The Prof was more than happy to oblige.

"That's right, you *don't* see and *won't* see any children. Not because there's a high infant mortality rate here... quite the contrary, none are ever born. There are no kids here, even though we have absolutely no form of birth control available, because the ice..." he motioned towards a specimen dish of the native bacteria in his hand, "makes humans sterile."

That was a real shocker for the two other scientists. When first recruited, the Prof had expected that the Confederation wanted the benefits of the immortality drug they could produce solely for military use; which would be fairly useless, as they would only have soldiers that would live longer using a drug on a daily basis at their expense. But with this side-effect, they certainly wouldn't be able to sell it to any off-planet colonists, whose main purpose was to get off Earth to forge a new start, find better jobs, and raise families.

There might be a few eccentrics who would want to extend their lifespan a few hundred years or so, but the tests he had made so far showed that any patient would be dependent on the drug on a daily basis. The fact that it made people irreversibly sterile would turn this whole immortality drug project into one big rotten lemon. Even artificial insemination programs would be useless if a woman was unable to carry the child and only the very, very rich could afford a special drug that needed to be kept in such a tightly controlled environment in order to keep the bacteria cultures alive. The Prof had done several such experiments that proved the native water of Earth was not a proper catalyst for the alien bacteria.

The Doc remembered the old dead core sample he had studied, and had never considered that the ice crystals of Europa were the only medium that the bacteria could survive in. Even though it caught him off guard and this news nearly trashed all his original theories, the Doc couldn't help but laugh out loud.

"Well, I guess this will teach those bastards! They are spending every last credit they have to finance this charade. I would love to see the look on Charlie's face when he finds out he can't sell his cash cow to anyone...

hah-ha," Doc chortled while scratching his head. It was Min who had the sense to bring the conversation back to reality.

"But if that is true, doesn't that mean that they will be killing all the inmates for nothing?" He stated flatly.

His words brought a harsh silence. The fact was, we were expecting the troopers to come storming the planet at any moment. It had been nearly six days ago via Earth time since Sarge had zapped out the orbiting satellites. That was certainly long enough to send a few star cruisers full of soldiers here by light drive. Once we got the solar cells charged up, we were going to have to work hard to save our own necks.

We really needed to get Rook into the communications room so that she could start adjusting the narrow band relays to transmit a mayday. Our hopes were riding on the slim chance that someone besides a Confederation starship was near enough to help us out before the clock ran out on us.

The three scientists finally puckered out from our long trip and the hours they had spent squabbling over their research, which thankfully, gave me the chance to get some much needed rest. I woke up several hours later to Sarah offering me some hot cocoa, for which I was extremely grateful.

"The solar cells have recharged and Voc is trying to bypass the door locks," Sarah informed me with a bright smile, while I warmed my hands on the steaming plastic mug, "Oh, and Roller wanted your help in the bay to move some of the cranes so he could clear the doorway to the other domes," She finished and patted me on the shoulder.

I'm usually quite grouchy when I first wake up, but I

decided not to grumble too much and savored my little cup of heaven. These long days and nights on this moon were starting to get on my nerves, and I could see how the Prof had gone a little crazy. I brought up the subject to the Doc, who took my sarcastic joke for a serious turn. He informed me that back in the ancient days of Rome and Greece, the life expectancy of an average Joe was only about 30 years of age. Which was sure young to be dying, but I could understand how life was a bit harsh way back then. According to the doctor, he and Min had both studied cases on the elderly population back when they were interns.

Their common theory was that; like our other internal organs, the human brain just wasn't built for such extended use. When one ages, your joints become brittle, skin and muscle tone decrease and your whole body wears away, and so does the brain. Now as he was figuring that the Prof was in the ballpark around 140+ years old, he was certainly willing to give his odd character some leeway. So he asked me to be patient with the Professor as well. Doc didn't have the proper equipment here to see what long term effects the ice fully had on bodily tissues, but he expected what it had done to the old man's internal organs was a good clue.

Thinking about it, he might have had a point. If in fact this youth drug did actually work, it mainly affected the epidermis exclusively. Even those few people who might take the medication for an extended time, say a hundred years or so, might look just fine on the outside, but their organs would still be deteriorating around the normal rate of aging. They might just keel over dead at any moment from a weakened heart or a decayed brain. That sure did take the spark out of the whole concept.

Of course, I certainly didn't hesitate to think that the Confederation would *actually* care about the long-term effects of this product; they were only in it for the down and dirty few trillion credits they could drum up from selling it. Which kind of made them no better than the drug dealers they were incarcerating, themselves.

I found Roller with his work gloves on, trying to free a rusted joint in one of the small mechanical cranes. The thing refused to budge, so he finally had to take a torch to it. Behind a load of barrels and other scrap material, we found a small storage locker under the hanging platform. The work took a while, because we refused to let the women help us clear the area to the portal, which had a large bold '**A-4**' painted across it.

Back near the lab at the door labeled '**A-1**', Voc had taken longer than expected trying to figure out the old touch-tone lock system and chose to hack into the memory chip to access the code. It turned out to be a simple three-digit sequence repeating itself: 111. He grumbled out loud over the idiocy of having a locking system for the doorways when you would consider that at the time this was built, there was no other living soul on the entire planet except for the survey team itself.

At first, the door refused to open for us, but in his exasperation, Voc gave it a stout kick which persuaded it to finish its unlocking cycle. The short hallway beyond led to the adjacent unit with a large '**A-2**' plastered across the doorway in bold letters. Voc tried the triple-1 sequence again on its panel, but it didn't work. He cursed out loud and was about to set out his tools again to pry open the panel when Sarah shoved passed him and hit three numbers on the keyboard. Voc stared at her in astonishment as the door slowly opened with the grinding of metal.

"How did you do that?" He asked.

"I've spent several years in a warehouse, and you have to consider that all this equipment was supplied by a mining company. Usually, just the simplest codes are used, so I figured I would give it a try... couldn't hurt," She motioned with a shrug of her shoulders.

"Yeah, but... how did you know the code?" Voc was trying to comprehend with his busy little brain.

"You're thinking about it too hard, Voc," she laughed, "the code to the 1st unit was 111, so doesn't it make sense that the code to the second dome would be triple 2? Especially with that big 'A2' printed on the door!"

Voc looked stunned for a moment. He had been trained in all the latest forms of advanced technology, which had *nothing* to do with simplicity. All he could do was grunt and roll his eyes at her.

Dome 2 seemed to have been the sleeping quarters for the survey staff. A maze of oval beds was lined throughout the room along with several more desks, empty footlockers, and bits of odd trash. Doc scoured the room until he found a locker with a specific nameplate attached to it. He rifled through a few scraps of old discarded notes he found there, written by the same team member whose old logbook he had studied back on Earth. It was very nostalgic the way he sat there on that bed, handling the old crumbled notes.

There was an old faded map of the complex attached to one wall. It showed all five dome units the way they had looked back before they were buried under the ice. The graph also showed an expanded view of the surrounding area and the locations where certain drilling sites were situated. Apparently there was a fairly large one located under dome A-5, but that was in the opposite direction from the cargo bay where we had entered. To their excitement, the chart also showed that the next dome over at A-3 was the Com-Center where all the communications relays were located.

Without giving a backward glance to Sarah, Voc quickly pressed the code 333 into the keypad. When nothing happened, he desperately tried again in vain. Sarah strode forward and patted him gently on the back in her friendly manner, but I could swear I saw a smirk flash across her face.

"We are still in dome two, so…" she slowly punched in 222 with the light tapping of her finger, and the door grudgingly opened to the linking corridor beyond. If Voc seemed a little defeated, he sure tried not to show it, but the three scientists all shared a secret glance and a light humored grin behind his back.

Rook strolled forward through the passageway to a thick metal door on the far end and quickly punched in 333 to the keypad to which the door cycled open with a sharp grind. The chamber beyond was frosted over at a greater degree than the other rooms we had seen, but all the equipment seemed pretty much intact. Roller went back to grab a portable heater as Rook and Voc began applying their skills to the antique apparatus. While the technicians were busy, everyone else went to check out the door that Roller and I had cleared earlier.

This portal was noticeably wider than the others, but Sarah suggested that this was probably to accommodate large supply crates for storage. We certainly didn't think that we would find anything usable like edible provisions, considering their age, and were probably all shipped out when the base was abandoned. We still had a decent supply of military rations from the shipwreck, but they were so bland it was like eating sawdust.

Sarah strolled up to the A-4 access door but was a bit dismayed to find two-panel locks, instead of one. She tried to set in the appropriate three-digit code on both of them but became discouraged when that tactic failed to work. I asked Roller if perhaps we should drag Voc back here to try to hack the lock for us, but he suggested that the first priority for our technician was to get the Communications systems operational for Rook. Doc, Min, and the Prof stood back, and waited for us to do something miraculous. However, Roller just shrugged his shoulders, grabbed a handy pipe from the deck, and then promptly jammed it into one of the keyboards.

This would not have been my first choice of action, but before I could say anything he had smashed the panel into a mess of broken buttons and flying sparks. Sarah and I shielded ourselves from the few errant electrical sparks that shot out, while Roller just stood there expectantly. Of course, nothing happened, and a look of guilt started to creep across his boyish face.

Well, there was no use in complaining now, but I still would have preferred a chance to dismantle the panel in a more civilized manner. Sarah asked the brute for a pair of pliers from his utility belt, and he solemnly obliged. The keypad itself used an old outdated two-poled conduit, so it wasn't too long after she played with the guts of wires until she found a way to short circuit the locking cycle.

The huge door hissed and groaned; lifting slowly up into the wall. As it rose, we could see that the hall beyond had been built much wider and set with a heavy metal grate flooring. When the thick mist had finally cleared, we were startled to find a large mechanical robot that completely blocked the corridor beyond. The thing sat on a set of evil-looking spiked wheels, which I can imagine would have been useful to tread on the ice. Its upper body was a chromed aluminum alloy and was fitted with a pair of crude arm-like appendages.

Braced high upon its shoulders was a large sensory egg, plated with gold to keep the orb from tarnishing.

"What the hell is that thing?" Doc shouted from behind as Roller and I took a step closer.

"It looks like an old multi-service unit used for moving cargo and equipment in the docking bay or out on the field; beats the hell out of using sled dogs, that's for sure!" Roller answered.

It was an awkward piece of oversized equipment, but then, such automatons might have been widely used on standard drilling operations a century ago. It sure was an eyesore. We moved a little closer to figure out just how we were going to drag this heap of metal out of the hallway when Sarah gave out a loud gasp of surprise and we all took a cautious step back.

The machine began to rattle from somewhere inside its hulking shell and its arms moved up and froze with a pair of dangerous-looking pincers pointing directly at us. Roller had smashed the controls to the door; so unfortunately, there was no way of closing it again. All I could do was stand there in a cold panic as a searing streak of light broke open across the face of its orb.

Automaton

We frantically stumbled over ourselves trying to evacuate the blocked corridor as the robot powered up. If the unpredictable thing lurched forward, it would certainly crush us under its spiked wheels. We couldn't even begin to presume what kind of final command programming it had been left with, so we didn't want to be within reaching distance of those sharp metal pincers. All three of the scientists literally fell over each other as they tried to flee down the stairway, while Roller made a lunge for the pipe he had used to smash the locking panel. Sarah and I backed up against the railing, holding on to each other as we almost fell off the platform.

As we all glanced back in stark fear, the thing rolled forward a few meters through the doorway and came to a sudden halt, accompanied by a few loud clanks and a dying whir. The light on its face-plate faded away and the robot powered down. The three scientists were all holding each other at the bottom of the stairwell as they gazed back up at the hulking machine with wide eyes. Roller was brave enough to tap the thing with the pipe, testing it warily, but nothing happened.

"Is it dead?" The Prof cried out with a tint of hope coloring his voice.

"Hah… not *dead*, just out of juice I would guess," Roller laughed, "These things run on old wet cell batteries, it sure gave us a jump, wouldn't you say!"

"But why did it come after us like that?" Doc inquired, "Was it programmed to protect the facility from the convicts?"

"Not likely," Sarah added, "this place was abandoned long before they even thought about using this moon as a prison planet. Most likely the cold preserved a trickle of juice in it after all these years, and the thing probably has a motion sensor in that brain box."

I was still shaking a bit; I didn't react well to being suddenly spooked like that. Roller and I took a closer look at the contraption, the slave droids we had nowadays weren't nearly as intimidating as this one was.

"Well, it's completely blocking the doorway now, how the hell are we going to move it out of the way?" I tried to ponder. Roller took the more direct approach by using his brute force first, and his brain second ...it was just something I noticed about him.

"*Uhg*," Roller groaned as he tried to drag the robot out, "...Damn! Those spiked wheels are caught in the metal grating, and it's too damn heavy."

I peered up at the two cargo cranes that were anchored in the bay, but they were used for hoisting supply boxes to the upper level and were nowhere near the portal.

"Tell you what, this thing runs on bipolar leads, so let's use one of the spare plasma cells from the buggy and get Voc to run a diagnostic on this thing when he's done in the communications room," I suggested. Roller nodded and headed out for the rover to grab a spare power cell, while Sarah kept a gentle hold on my arm, which I didn't mind in the least.

Doc went back to the communications dome to let our technicians know what we had found, while Sarah and I jimmied opened the access panel on the robot. I pried out the giant core battery, which I swore must have weighed 50 kilos, and dropped it onto the grating with a thud. Roller came back shortly with the fist-sized plasma cell, so I just set it inside the spacious compartment, realizing that there would be plenty of extra room to store something else in there. I wasn't about to hot-wire it up until Voc did a systems check on this thing and gave us the 'Okay' that it wouldn't short circuit and fry itself.

Both Min and Doc went back to browse over the Professor's notes in the lab while the rest of us decided to check in on how the communications repair was coming. The room was much warmer now since the heaters had melted the frost, which had left a few puddles of water scattered about the room. Rook was at the console and gave me a quick smile as I came in; Voc was waist-deep under one of the opened panels. He yelled out to Rook to switch to a different transformer, and she turned the dial up as a crackle of static came over the air.

She adjusted the transmitter over to several narrow-band frequencies. We stood there expectantly as she tested the microphone.

"Mayday! Mayday! If you are receiving this signal, please respond," but she was only met with static. After making a few more adjustments she switched to a broadband channel and we could only hope that the ice outside had not completely ruined the antenna dish. Rook tried to pinpoint a few bits of random noise that came in, but I realized it would be difficult to try and grab anybody's attention on such an old megahertz frequency. Voc kept working the wires under the console until we caught a faint reply.

"*Krrrtt~* This is Starseer mining command on Phobos responding to a mayday call. Please repeat your transmission, over." We all looked about hopefully as Rook responded.

"We read you Phobos, come in, this is a mayday call

from Echo, Uniform, Romeo, Oscar, Papa, Alpha, over."
A few minutes of dead air followed, and Rook thought
that we had lost him. We stood there in long silence,
hoping to hell that they weren't reporting this
transmission to the Confederation. A few waves of static
hit the speaker as they finally came back on.

"*Krrrtt~* Echo Uniform, please give us your telemetry
so we can zero in on your signal, over." Rook just raised
up her hands in aggravation, as we really didn't have any
such data on hand. When Sarge skipped out on us, he
took the stellar communicator that would have provided
our coordinates, but this old equipment was lacking a
few technical nuts and bolts.

"Phobos command, we are Confederation operatives on
J2, repeat, Juliet Two... We are in need of emergency
assistance, over," she stated, hoping this would grab their
attention.

"*Krrrtt~* Echo Uniform, you are using an outdated
mining band channel. We will promptly contact the
Confederation to respond to your distress call, over."

Holy crap! That was certainly the last thing that we
wanted. Voc slid out from underneath the panel, while
desperately shaking his head at Rook who had just
realized her mistake.

"Uh, Negative Phobos, repeat, Negative. We have an
urgent message for your post; please give us someone in
charge at your facility, over." There was another long
moment of quiet static and we were all wondering if they
might just report this conversation to the Confederation
anyway, thinking we might just be a bunch of inmates
who had stumbled across a working transmitter and were
trying to con our way onto a rescue ship. Finally another
voice broke over the air.

"*Krrrtt*~ This is O'Neil, Starseer Director of Operations for Phobos Mining. We have verified your signal coming from Juliet Two, what is your status? Over."

I was quite impressed how Rook handled the rest of the conversation; since I could imagine if I was in the same shoes as Mr. O'Neil, I would have just brushed it all off as a hoax transmission from a bunch of convicts. Sarah went back to grab the Doc and Min, and all of us except the Prof introduced ourselves over the air.   Rook informed them that the Sentry satellite system had been destroyed and the Confederation upper brass was planning to exterminate the colony prisoners.

We realized it was a hard pill to swallow, but we tried to wait patiently as O'Neil took an hour off air to discuss the situation with his board. It was even hard for me to accept the truth of our position. Would anyone believe us before it was too late?

When O'Neil came back on the speaker, he stated that they did in fact have a planetary chart on record showing the location of the old survey base on Europa, and would send a cargo vessel with armed personnel to pick us up. We were all pleased to hear this, but he made it clear that they would only retrieve the seven of us. The Prof was more than a trifle upset to hear this, but we assured him that we would debate the matter when the rescue ship touched down. Even from Phobos, the asteroid moon of Mars, it would still take them nearly three Earth days to reach us. So we had to make plans to stick to our guns and hide here at the base, hoping that the Confederation ships wouldn't spot us before then.

This upset the Prof even more, because the military cruisers that were sent to execute the inmates would be here anytime now, and that still left them 72 hrs to do their dirty work and round up or slaughter whoever they happened to find. Roller agreed that he and the Prof should take the rover back to the shantytown where they had met the Prof, to warn Turvel and the rest of the convicts about the situation at hand.

Personally, I disagreed with this plan, considering how unpredictable that maniac could be. Even the Prof agreed that Turvel might not believe his story and string them both up for desertion. This would also present a problem if he and his Raiders should decide to hold a welcoming party at the survey base when our rescue ship arrived. The cargo shuttle might just decide to turn around and head back without us.

I agreed to take charge while Roller headed out to act as ambassador. We unloaded the majority of the hardware and weapons from the rover, but left one crate from the crashed recon ship in the back of the vehicle in case they needed evidence to show Turvel. Roller was taking a huge risk by doing this, but he had a heavy conscience that urged him to at least give the prisoners a fighting chance. We saw them off topside as they sped away across the frozen tundra, all the while keeping a wary eye out for signs of Military ships against the harsh red sky.

Voc finally had a chance to give the slave-bot we found a thorough inspection, and ran a simple diagnostic on its core programs. He laughed when he saw it, if there was a way to get it back to Earth, it could certainly fetch a few credits as an antique. He detached a single channel remote from the interior; its brain wasn't exactly an AI, but instead responded to rudimentary voice commands. After checking that the remote was still functional, Voc handed it to me for safekeeping.

He had to bypass some internal circuitry before hooking

up the plasma cell; otherwise he would have fried its brain core. This time the thing powered up a lot stronger than it had before; and its internal display went through a series of primary systems checks. I had to get some maintenance oil used for our rifles to put on its internal gears, just so it could function properly. Voc pointed out that I only had to speak into the remote, but suggested I should try to keep my instructions fairly simple.

"Um... Robot, please move out of the doorway," I spoke into the device.

The thing rattled slightly, which bothered me, because I thought I had fixed that little annoyance with the oil. Its response was garbled a bit at first through its external speaker, until something fried and it went silent. Voc and I had thought it had broken down again, but the robot sprang to life and began to back away down the corridor. When it came to a standstill, Voc went up and opened its panel again to view the internal diagnostic display.

"Its speaker must have burned out because the plasma cell was pumping out too much power. Either that, or it's just ruined from age, but the response is shown here on the interior console, see," Voc pointed out as I took a look inside. Old-fashioned diode lights showed that most of the systems were functional, but unfortunately there was no way to repair the installed speaker. Inside the small compartment I could see that the display panel registered the words: 'COMMAND PERFORMED' across its tiny single-line screen.

"Uh... robot, that was the wrong way. Move out into the cargo bay, slowly please," I spoke into the remote while eyeing Voc. The machine took a long moment to think the commands over and lurched forward suddenly into the bay. We all jumped out of the way of its spiked tires accordingly as it made its way down the adjacent ramp and into the center of the cargo room. Voc went over to review its internal display again and made a few adjustments.

"Hmm... well Jim, it seems the bot here is delaying because you're using excessive words in your instructions," he related. I just gave him an odd glance and shrugged my shoulders.

"What do you mean?" I inquired, a little dumbfounded.

"Well, it's appears to be having a hard time processing the word 'please' and it is referring to its serial number for a name." Voc related.

Sarah went up to take a look inside the panel, "Its ID number for this automaton is: SAM-662-28. I guess try to call it that or something other than 'Robot' if you can.

"That's a little hard to remember, how about just 'Sam' for short?" I blurted back. I had never had exclusive control over a droid before. Sarah and Voc flashed each other a short glance, while Sarah replied with an amusing idea that even the technician approved of.

"Eh, how about you name him Charlie," she smiled, "that way you can order *him* around for a change."

I chuckled at that one; it would be an ironic name to use, but why the hell not!

"Hmm, let's see, (I poked my head inside the panel to read its serial number) SAM-662-28, you will respond to all commands from now on as 'Charlie', confirm your orders," The bot took an achingly long moment to process the information, and then a message crossed the screen, reading: 'CONFIRMED'. At that, Voc sealed up the panel again and we decided to take a look down the cold mysterious corridor to see what curiosities the other adjacent domes might hold.

The portal at the end of the passage didn't have the same A-4 painted across the door we had expected to find, but Sarah quickly punched in the triple 4 code into the panel and the lock cycled open. The room beyond was frozen over to a greater extent than the Com center had been while icicle-like structures could be seen branching out from several of the stacked bins. Doc and the Prof studied these strange formations in detail and discovered that they were growing out of old food crates that had been contaminated by the native bacteria. The rest of the supply boxes littering the room held various mechanical gears used for machinery and core analysis.

Odd types of drill bits were lying about, and Voc even found a few extra interesting accessories for our 'Charlie-bot' to use. These were extra limb attachments for the robot that must have been designed for a variety of uses. Voc picked up one of these and examined it closely.

"This could come in handy, very useful indeed," he murmured with a nod of his head.

"What is it, Voc?" I asked curiously.

"Oh, this arm gear must have been used for a variety of analyzing purposes, such as ice content, radiation detection, etc. However, with the higher amps from the plasma cell we installed, this little toy could be turned into a decent defense weapon," he smiled back, "We could certainly use all the help we can get when the Troopers come knocking on our door."

Voc went back to the bay to see if he might be able to fool around with the robot's internal circuitry and reinstall the new limb on Charlie. The doctor was busy discussing the ice crystal growths with the other two scientists as they gently extracted a few samples from the breached crates so they could bring them back to the lab.

Rook was still in the Communications room monitoring the airwaves, so Sarah and I figured we could explore the last dome while everyone else was preoccupied.

We passed through the door at the opposite end of the room and into the frozen corridor beyond. I had to brush away the heavy frost covering the last door to A-5 with my glove so that I could see the markings. It was a little odd how this one was so completely iced over. When Sarah punched in the appropriate code, the green light came on but the door remained frozen shut. We had to go back and grab a few portable heaters and face them at the door, hoping that they would defrost the locking pins. While we waited, Sarah and I worked over our supplies list to partition out our heavy weaponry in case we might need it to defend the base.

Voc finally got around to finishing the install of the new limb on Charlie, and he asked me to give it a test run on one of the storage crates.

"I recalibrated the cycling of the exterior sensor, now it builds up an electric charge that can be dissipated on an object ...just make sure it's kept away from the bots shell, otherwise, it might accidentally zap itself," Voc offered with a self-satisfied grin.

I pulled out the remote from my jacket pocket and gave a glance over to Voc, "Uh, so what do I tell it to do?"

"Just tell it to scan the box. That's what its newly attached analyzer arm was made for," he replied.

"Okay, here goes," I began, and Voc took a few steps back to clear the test crate. "Charlie, scan the box in front of you," A thin streak of light came on across the golden orb atop its upper stem, but otherwise, nothing happened. A bit confused, Voc stepped forward for a moment to open the panel and peeked inside.

"Oops, I forgot the external speaker was shot. It did in fact scan the crate, but only with its upper orb sensors in the brain box instead of using the arm attachment. Hmm... let's see, try ordering it to *analyze* the box instead," he suggested. I did so, and the bot lurched forward and extended its probe. The tip began to glow a bright blue, which I figured was the electrical surge building up, then a large ball of plasma energy grew out from the tip. Instantly, a crackle of blinding white electrical arcs shot out from the glowing orb and scorched the container with a potent discharge. All the metal nubs and joints on the crate sparked violently, and the plasma ball instantly dissipated.

When we went up to examine the box, we saw that the joints had actually been melted. This sure wasn't something we wanted toy around with! Voc grinned in satisfaction as I put the remote away. There, of course, had to be some other uses we could put this machine to, perhaps it had an embedded database that I could access to bring up some of the history on this place. I strolled over and opened up the maintenance panel while I grabbed for my remote. This way I could read Charlie's response when I made a request.

"Charlie, what equipment is in dome 5?" A message flashed across the screen on its one-line display, so I had to read quickly.

<Manta Drill and Trans Unit>

"What is a Manta drill?" I asked into the remote.

<Manta Drill is a specialized robotic device for drilling ice> was all it read, which was a bland enough answer I could have guessed on my own.

I went over to grab Sarah, and we went back up the corridor to see how the defrosting was coming along.

The door was now covered with beads of water that had failed to dry for some reason. I wasn't too keen on understanding the bizarre reactions of the ice crystals on this moon as Doc was, so this didn't seem too odd to me at first. The door still wouldn't budge, even though the electrical panel showed that it had verified the unlocking command.   Being naturally impatient to satisfy my curiosity, I ordered Charlie to open the door.

Sarah and I heard it whir to life and we watched the robot lurch back up the ramp, through the supply room and into the corridor towards our position. It wasn't until the clamoring automaton was halfway upon us that I realized that we were both trapped between it and the doorway with the bulk of the huge machine barreling at us on its deadly spiked wheels. As it was coming steadily upon us, I tried to juggle with the remote so I could command it to stop, and could only hope that its internal sensors would detect us before it ran us over, and I began to fear that they might not be functioning at all. Sarah backed up flat against the wall and gave me a scared glance.

"Make it stop, Jim!" Sarah pleaded in a nervous pitch.

"Give me a second," I barked back, "I, I just wanted the bot to open the door..." I replied anxiously as I fumbled with the remote, the bot came to a sudden halt with only a half meter to spare, trapping us between its hulking metallic mass and the frozen door to our backs. It shot out its left arm, and a small gear popped up out of its pincer. Charlie then extended its arm into a socket at the corner of the door, just a few centimeters from my head. The robot's movements were so fast, it made me flinch.

We heard the gears crank behind the hull panel, and the door groaned loudly as it slowly opened into the room beyond. The chamber was a half glass dome, but even though it had been buried in the ice, the layer covering it was thin enough at the top to let in an ample amount of daylight. We immediately noticed that there was a high level of humidity in this chamber, despite the frozen icicles hanging from the ceiling. There were numerous tubes and pipes lining the floor, all laced to a central hub lying within the middle of the room, which was covered with a huge circular grate. We walked inside and brought in our portable heaters that had nearly been crushed by Charlie. Among the numerous consoles lining the room, there was also a strange-looking couch set at the far end of the chamber. Oddly shaped plates were attached to its base, and as I approached to inspect it I could see that it had a customized control panel set neatly in front of it.

We picked our way over the tubes littering the floor to take a closer look at the machinery, wondering why nothing here resembled anything like a coring drill. A display near a blinking light on the console simply read the word 'BREACH', and not quite understanding this ridiculous surveyor's lingo wasn't helping much either. Sarah took a seat in the plush couch that was rimmed with chromed blue steel; it had a sleek retro design that kept me wondering about its function.

"Hey Jim, come take a look at this," Sarah called, pointing to the vid-screen at the lower console of the couch. I crawled in next to her and looked at the display of dials and buttons that lit up the interior. What caught my attention was that there was a gyroscope displayed in one corner, and I wondered why a console chair would need a leveling unit. Most of the glowing buttons were blue or green, except for a flickering red light labeled: 'RETRACT'. I learned in the Academy about how 'blinking red lights' most usually presented serious problems, but apparently, Sarah had skipped that class. Before I could figure out what exactly the flashing light was indicating too, Sarah reached out and hit the button *while* she was uttering, "Why is this one blinking?"

We both froze in our seats for the few milliseconds it took for a glass shield to shoot out and encapsulate us in the console couch. Several of the other previously darkened indicators started flashing wildly, and the vid-screen in front of Sarah powered on to display a wire-frame map showing some sort of device being drawn up a long tube. The floor around us started to rumble and we looked at each other in shock; just then the circular grate in the center of the room cycled open to expose a great black hole lying beneath. In a flurry of mist and shaved ice, out the cavity came a grinding metal machine with spinning sharp blades surrounding its main body.

Through the spray of ice that landed on the shield, we watched as the drill blades ceased revolving and a mechanical arm extended from the ceiling above the chasm to connect with the robotic body. It then retracted the whole unit back up into the ceiling, clearing the gaping hole exposed beneath. Just then, I was trying to remember what the Charlie-bot had mentioned about this room. Something about a Manta drill and Trans unit, that thing on the ceiling had been the drill, but what was that reference for a 'transportation vehicle' the robot had referred to?

As Sarah and I were trying desperately to find a lever or switch to open up the glass lid, we got a scary surprise as a mechanized rod shot out from beneath the console and positioned itself between my legs. The end of the device flapped open into a handle with a button, while another similar arm shot up to my left. It took me a moment to figure out what the hell was going on. Sarah was staring at me, wondering what these gadgets were.

"Oh god …this is a cockpit!" I muttered to myself, and on that cue we felt the couch shudder and whir to life.

"How do we open the canopy?" Sarah screeched back, but a majority of the buttons on the console only showed various bizarre symbols instead of words to describe their function. This confusing annoyance thoroughly disoriented me for a moment, so I tried pushing a few that looked promising …and oh boy, what a mistake that was. Sarah panicked as our steel carriage edged forward on its tracks, carrying us towards the dark chasm stationed at the center of the room.

"Make it stop, Jim, get us out of here!" She shrieked.

"I'm trying, shit, I'm trying…!" I screamed back at her, but all of the buttons I pushed after that just turned dark after being depressed. Nothing seemed to work, we were hopelessly trapped within the strange craft. We stared out glumly at the golden-faced robot in the doorway, which looked back at us dolefully with his single laser eye as we approached the dark void. I thought about asking him to help us as I fumbled for the remote in my pocket.

Just as I found it, Sarah's hysterical scream broke my concentration as the vessel tilted over the breach of the chasm and sent us plummeting into the darkness below.

Confrontation

Roller never thought he would find himself over half a billion kilometers from home trying to protect a bunch of hoodlums from the Confederation. He had gotten all his weaponry skills from serving time in the military, but there was just something missing in modern warfare that made him become offended to combat that usually consisted of nothing more than bombing the enemy at a safe distance... there was no honor involved there. For being such a large hulking warrior with honed combat skills, he had a soft spot for getting in the other guys shoes. In a fight, this seasoned recruit could easily snap any assailant's neck in a nanosecond, but personally, he had to be presented with a damn good reason to do so.

He was well aware that a good majority of the criminals incarcerated on J6 were the worst of the worst, only having being sent here because Earth no longer carried a death sentence. But there were still others here who did not fully fit that profile. In the past few decades, the Confederation had secretly lowered its standards for convict deportation to this prison planet and a lot of *not-so-rotten* folks had been dumped here as well.

Roller understood that a good percentage of the felons that ended up here were merely products of their environment. A century ago, Earth had turned into a cesspool of citizens fighting to survive any way they could, and several cities were overwhelmed by years of indiscriminate chaos. The Confederation had sprung out of the social turmoil and sought to establish some form of order, and helped curb the senseless violence. Society itself had been bursting at the seams, and had suffered all the symptoms that come with a gross overpopulation problem. There just wasn't enough room to keep people from bumping shoulders in the urban cities. It was human nature to be self-sufficient and to provide some sort of security for one's own survival …it just so happens that convicts were a breed that didn't consider the generally accepted rules of conformity and common respect as most civilians did. In a world of chaos, there were no rules.

He had seen his share of peace officers who indulged themselves with several forms of corruption, but Roller usually kept quiet about his prior service in the Confederation. He had been blacklisted and reassigned time and again for being a whistleblower with too many ethics. He fully suspected that if he had been of any smaller stature, he would certainly have been a victim of some immediate form of malicious reprisal. Then, of course, that's probably how Lt. Charles had made sure he wound up here, providing a known dissenter in their ranks with a one-way ticket to nowhere.

He hated himself at this moment, knowing he should've been able to smell a rat like Sarge a parsec away. Well, at least he could try to make a difference now and help the inmates understand the full scope of what the Council had in store for them.

The Prof had remained silent during most of their ride, only to mutter to himself occasionally about any random subject that might cross his mind. Understanding that the poor fellow might be suffering from a form of dementia, the soldier tried to humor the Prof with some philosophical topics. Once he got on a roll though, the old man had a habit of taking over the conversation.

"You know, Turvel is just one of a hundred power hungry gimps I've seen run through this place over the years, so don't expect him to be too receptive," the old man advised.

"I'm sure you're right Professor, but I was thinking that if we play into his appetite for control, we might be able to convince him to take some action," Roller added.

The Prof shifted in his seat, looking the giant man in the eyes, "But what reason does he have to give a damn about the rest of the inmates… he might just want to save his own ass. What are we going to ask him to do? Run and hide? Fat chance, *hmph*!"

This did present a problem. Roller didn't stop to realize that most of the convicts he would run into would lack the common ethics of character to help their fellow man. The Prof was right, the individual inmates would most likely try to save their own skins without any concern for the others …this was a dog eat dog world after all.

As they approached the outskirts of the complex, Roller parked the rover behind a few small dunes and proceeded on foot with the Prof in the lead. For his own protection, he hefted a quad barrel pulse rifle slung over his shoulder. There was notably much less activity now than he had seen before, but there were still a few wandering souls who took one look at him and his big gun, and went scurrying for cover. When they finally reached the main building where Turvel had detained them, a score of red-armored guards rushed out of the main door with crude spears and long knives in hand. Automatic reflexes kicked in, and Roller dropped his rifle to the ready.

"Hold it right there!" One of them demanded.

The Professor came forward to talk to the head guard and motioned over to Roller once during their hushed conversation, while the rest of the surrounding goons eyed the huge soldier nervously. Finally, the head guard came forward a few steps shy of the armed warrior.

"The Professor says you want a private meeting with Turvel, and that he will vouch for you, but you have to leave your gun outside," he demanded. Roller only grinned at his proposal.

"The hell I will! You tell Turvel to return my pistol and I'll think about it," he replied flatly.

The guard stalled for a moment, realizing that he didn't want to continue an argument with a hulking giant bearing heavy artillery. He gave a disgruntled sneer and headed off back into the building while the other guards kept an eye on him as they muttered among themselves.

After a long moment, the same man came back outside, motioning them both to come in. They kept Roller at a respectable distance as he tromped past, keeping wary of where those four shiny silver barrels where pointed. Turvel was sitting in the same captain's chair looking very weary, as though he had just woken up. He still had Roller's old handgun slung in his belt.

"Well Rookie, you best have a damn good reason for coming back here. I don't put up with deserters or other grunts trying to take over my turf," he warned, "I better like your excuse, or even that new toy of yours isn't going to save your ass in here," Upon that cue, a dozen more red guards poured in out of the shadows to circle him. Roller was thinking maybe this guy wasn't so stupid after all. He kept his eyes locked on Turvel without a mere flinch.

"I don't know how long you've been trapped on this rock," Roller grinned while patting his monstrous gun casually, "but this little baby is a quad barrel C-74 fully articulate military issue pulse rifle," He then nodded his head to either side, indicating to the guards, yet keeping his cold stare on the man in the captain's seat directly in front of him.

"And..?" Turvel yawned, unimpressed.

Roller hit some hidden button on the trigger housing and the four barrels rapidly scissored themselves in one quick automated motion and instantly returned to their original position. This caused all the guards to jump suddenly to their unease, only Turvel kept his cool, but his eyes did widen ever so slightly.

"Which means, I could clean out half of this room with one shot, and take out the other half before you could say *ouch*," Roller finished, but his grin quickly disappeared into a thin serious line, which Turvel seemed to notice immediately. Without saying, all the surrounding guards took a cautious step back.

"So then, why exactly are you here?" Turvel asked uncomfortably while shifting in his seat.

"I won't bullshit you, because we don't have time," he replied, "Several squadrons of armed Confederation troopers will be landing here soon and claim to be escorting all of the prisoners to another penitentiary off-planet. But that will just be a ploy to get you to cooperate as they round you all up like cattle to be slaughtered."

Turvel huffed in disbelief, "Why should the Law give a crap about us and go to the trouble? Furthermore, what the hell could we do about it anyway?"

Roller nodded to the Prof, and he quickly filled Turvel in on the details about how they sabotaged the Sentry and were interested in the effects of the ice, and how the military wanted to exploit this frozen moon. At hearing this, Turvel let out a boisterous laugh and pushed the Professor aside; being brave enough to come within a few steps of the armed GI.

"Hah, figures! I always said the Confederation was the worst sort of mafia. Now they think they can just mop us away like we never existed... the bastards!" He took a few slow steps back to his chair, then turned around. "So why the hell should I trust you?"

"Because we are in the same boat," Roller confessed.

"Perhaps, but what's going to keep them from whacking everyone on this planet ...besides you and your little toy gun there?" Turvel spat while gesturing towards the assault rifle, "In case you hadn't noticed, there ain't a lot of places for us to hole up on this ball of ice."

"I'm just trying to warn you that you shouldn't believe what they say when the troopers land," Roller sighed with annoyance.

"I damn well ain't going to run!" Turvel cut in.

"You may not have to," Roller hesitated while scanning the room of men wielding pitiful handmade weapons and spears. They wouldn't stand a chance against armed troopers for more than a nanosecond. "I have coordinates for a Confederation recon ship that crashed several clicks from here, it was full of weaponry. If you take your Raider skids there, you can arm yourselves with whatever you can find at the crash site. At least it will give you a fighting chance."

Turvel glared at him with suspicion, "Now just how did a Confederation ship come to crash topside, hmm?"

"The orbiting sentinel shot it down," Roller shrugged.

"I thought you said that damn machine was destroyed!" Turvel retorted, not really believing that a military ship would be attacked by its own security device.

"From what I know, it was a reconnaissance ship that came to scan the surface, but that was before the Sentry was eliminated. I've seen the ship and the weapons myself," the soldier finished, knowing that arming these convicts was one of the worst ideas he had ever had. Turvel was a bit too eager to get his hands on the guns, and demanded that Roller turn over the map he carried. Still though, Turvel kept up his suspicion until he finally asked why Roller; an ex-confederation soldier, would even bother to help a bunch of convicts.

"The Confederation has become corrupt to the core. Perhaps some of you were even dumped here on misdemeanor charges that had been falsely trumped up, but that was because the Council has been forging their quota's to keep their budgets high for the trillions of credits they've been extorting from the global tax system. Personally, I don't think getting put on ice is fair or justifiable punishment …there has to be a better way."

His words struck a note with the occupants of the room as a few of the guards broke into a subdued agreement, only Turvel failed to reciprocate their approval.

"Even if we fight back, we would all still be sorely outnumbered. We have no real chance of fending off a legion of military personnel," he turned around and retook his seat, "Perhaps they *are* just coming down to take us off this hellhole of a planet, and relocate us someplace fairly decent. Who knows what public policies have been initiated back on Earth, maybe the social council lobbied for giving us better treatment."

Roller couldn't understand Turvel's abrupt change of attitude; was there something he had missed? The Prof looked just as surprised by this sudden tilt of the conversation and gave him an incredulous glance. Roller swayed for a moment, not knowing if this fellow fully understood their predicament.

"Defending yourselves is your *only* chance, you'll be massacred if you don't," Roller's flat statement was almost pleading for Turvel to grasp a measure of sanity.

"Or maybe that's only what you *want* us to think," Turvel's sly grin crept upon his face as he leaned back into his chair, "Now, what do you make of all this nonsense, Mr. Cross?" A silhouette crept into the shadow of the doorway while Turvel gestured to the stranger. The man's raspy voice was almost recognizable.

"He is obviously a mole," The fellow in the shadows offered with a bitter chuckle, "My opinion is that he was sent down here to persuade you to attempt to start a prison riot, which would give the Confederation no other choice but to retaliate. Which of course, the military would love for us to do, so they could have an excusable reason to execute us on the spot. If we cooperate, then they have to abide by standard Terran laws and we can all get off this god-forsaken ice moon," he finished with a raspy strain lingering in his voice.

The man they called Cross slowly stepped forward, half out of the shadows, and Roller could see the fresh horrid scar that ran across his neck down the length of his chest that betrayed his affliction.

"As I said before, the Confederation is coming here to evacuate the inmates to take them back to Earth," the scarred man gave a warped grin. As the fellow strode forward into the dim light, Roller's eyes widened in shock. What the hell was Sarge doing here!

Under the Ice

Sarah's terrified scream nearly burst my eardrums as we plummeted into the abyss. I had never actually thought about how prepared I was for meeting my own death until this moment. Most people might pray, or have their life flash before their eyes. Personally, the only thing I could think of was; *whelp, this is the end of me...*

I could have probably outmatched Sarah's shriek by a few decibels, but at the moment I couldn't even breathe. Suddenly, there were several short electrical bursts which surrounded our steel carriage, and our fall decreased dramatically. I turned my head and watched in dread as fiery blue electrical arcs shot out from tiny rods on the sides of the vehicle while the shaft of ice briefly lit up around us. One thing was for certain, our descent was beginning to slow.

Sarah eased her hysterics to a series of yelps; which died down quietly as our fall decreased even more as the electrical rods became more active. Logic told me that the tiny ship we were in should have at least bumped the edges a few times, but it seemed now that our fall was being precisely controlled by some means. I was an aeronautics engineer, but I sure as hell had never encountered anything like this.

Sarah brought my attention back to the screen in front of us with an exaggerated motion by pointing with her rigid finger and looking desperately into my eyes. The monitor showed a wire-frame display of our ship and the surrounding tunnel. Something that appeared to be a large flat green disk was coming upon us fast.

"Oh god, we're going to hit bottom," Sarah yelped.

There was nothing we could do, and no time to think. All I could manage was to grab Sarah's hand as she clung tightly onto mine. Our free-fall came to a sudden end with an automated series of electric flashes outside the ship; then we hit the water.

"Oh my god, we're under the ice," I muttered in disbelief as a frail chuckle of relief escaped my lips. Just then, bright floodlights came on all over the ship and the Manta continued its journey through the tube of ice underwater.

"This ...this is a submarine," Sarah exclaimed lightly, still unbelieving. I looked at the screen again, and this time a thick turquoise line was coming up the screen towards us, but I didn't know what to think of it.

"Sarah, brace yourself!" I warned while nodding over to the screen. She gave a short whine and bit her lip. Not believing what I was seeing, through the glass canopy I could make out a faint blue light up ahead like a lone beacon in the darkness. We were left spellbound as we passed the final breach of the tunnel.

Our ship looped down into a vast underground ocean. Somehow, great cracks of light pierced down from the surface. The water was slightly foggy, so our visibility was hampered. We were stunned and stared in wonder at the sight before us. Glinting rays of soft light came down in long shafts from the ceiling of ice above us for as far as we could see. We sat there in silent awe for a moment till Sarah asked the question of the hour.

"Jim, can you pilot this thing?" Sarah inquired.

I could only look forlornly at the pair of hand controls for a long moment and then grabbed them to find they were no longer frozen. I tested their functions with the slightest of care.

"Um, well, I've actually never piloted a sub before, but let's give it a try," the fact was, I had piloted many airships and even a handful of small spaceworthy personnel carriers, but that was back when my father was still alive. It had been his job to inspect starcraft during construction and testing, and a few times he took me along for the ride.

I soon discovered this Manta sub was a whole different animal as I had to remember that these things worked on a type of ballast, similar to lighter-than-air ships. I tipped the controls once forward and we almost went crashing up into the solid ice ceiling above us. Out of nervous reaction, I quickly pulled the controls the other way and we went diving far below.

"Hmm, well the controls are reversed from what I'm used too, but the handle by the seat seems to act like a collective pitch or ballast. Hell, Sarah, I don't know ...just hang on!"

What was bothering me like a bad itch at the back of my mind was that I was wondering how the hell sunlight could reach this far below the surface. After all, the estimates I had read on all the reports had said that the ice cap of Europa was at least 50 kilometers thick... but it certainly didn't seem like we had actually dropped that far. I would have guessed we had traveled far less than a tenth of that distance, but I couldn't be certain.

I had no idea how to read the symbols on the screen for an accurate measurement, and I sure as hell wasn't going to go pushing any more buttons, fearing that I might accidentally open the cockpit shield and drown us both.

The real question was; how do we get ourselves out of this mess? So I asked Sarah to look around for some sort of manual, instructions, or anything that might have been left in the cockpit, but she couldn't find anything. The glowing vid-screen on the panel was our only friend at the moment, and I was hoping it would give us some clue how to return the ship back to the surface as the manta drill had when it had first retracted.

Suddenly, I remembered the two-way communicator radio that was clipped to my belt. I quickly whipped it out and handed it to Sarah. She tried to call out, but there was only a dull wisp of static.

"Nothing… there is just too much ice in the way. Jim, how are we going to get back?" She pleaded, and I could see the welling of a tear in her eyes.

"I don't know Sarah …I don't know," was all I could manage to say.

A green light came on under the console in front of Sarah just as a row of bright dots appeared on the screen. One by one they disappeared like a countdown, and then the controls abruptly jerked out of my hands, scraping on my fingers.

"What's going on?" Sarah demanded as the sub began a steep controlled dive as it apparently switched into autopilot. A large yellow button started blinking slowly on the console in front of me, but I could not decipher the archaic symbol it brandished, and you can bet I wasn't about to touch it.

A series of guidance beacons began to display on the screen, though we could see no such corresponding lights outside. They appeared in sequence, like an underwater road guiding our way. Wherever we were going, we had no control over it. There was nothing we could do.

The water became increasingly murkier the lower we sank. I couldn't understand what form of sedimentary silt was being kicked up from the bottom to thicken the water like this. Sarah was the first to point out what looked like tiny jellyfish, but as we plunged deeper these little creatures dramatically increased in size. I could hardly make out their details until a large one startled us as it hit our shield and slid past. I'm no biologist, but I would swear the thing looked like a one-celled amoeba; they were almost flat with a crimson center that reflected a rainbow of colors within our spotlights.

These slowly became more numerous, until whole clouds of these creatures flowed around us in the turbulence. A great dark shadow loomed towards us from below and glided past our ship, then another. Sarah and I looked on as these midnight-black objects flowed silently past us through the clouds of amoeba.

In a sudden breach, we cleared the living current and saw clearly what these ebony formations were. Like something out of a colossal rock display, enormous crystalline frameworks towered above the ocean floor below like sunken skyscrapers. We were left in awe as our sub flitted through great arcs and branches of the black crystal, down through enormous forests of dark glass.

Before we even had a clue that we had reached our destination, the sub came to a sudden halt. A few more of the hieroglyphic buttons flashed momentarily and the sub sank gently to the bottom. Even the ocean floor here had no silt, no sand; it was all made of the same solid ebony glass-like material. Then, all was still.

"Now what?" Sarah exclaimed, as we peered around, but could see nothing that could explain why the sub had chosen this spot to expire. I was beginning to get a little claustrophobic and wondered if this was the end of our joy ride, where we would be left to rot far beyond anyone's ability to reach us at this depth. Most likely we would run out of air long before we would die from starvation.   There was always the dreaded console buttons, but I wouldn't dare consider fiddling with them in light of the trouble it had already gotten us into.

The minutes of silence dragged on as Sarah and I exchanged looks of despair. Then quite suddenly, all the power to the console went dead. I would have become frantically concerned about that but noticed that our spotlights still remained on.

"Oh… my… God…" Sarah stuttered, "what is that?"

I looked in the direction our sub was facing, and one by one, tiny lights came on in the distant darkness as they slowly revealed the silhouette of some sort of archaic construction. Ever so slowly, our sub began to glide forward. Whatever this object was, we were about to get a closer look.

"Wait, Sarah…" I stumbled across my words, "this looks man-made!"

"But how is that possible Jim, the Confederation reports never said anything about…" she started to contend.

"Yeah, yeah, I know!" I cut her off, "See those tubes, and bulkhead bracings? Those are old structural designs," I explained. The only thing that bothered me was how in the hell was it built this far underwater, and secondly, why had there been absolutely no mention about it in the reports. Dr. Brendan, of all people, should have known about this structure from his thorough studies of all the archived data.   That is, unless such data had been purposefully purged or censored from the files.

Our sub proceeded into a small dimly lit tube and docked. A whir of hidden motors could be heard echoing in the water as a thick door behind us sealed shut. Slowly, the water began to be drained out of the cell our tiny ship was now occupying. The whole process was achingly slow.

I was having second thoughts about leaving the safety of our ship as the last of the ocean water was pumped away. There wasn't much choice in the matter, as our shield instantly slid back to let in a horridly cold draft of air. It was breathable but had a funny smell to it, a sickly-sweet stench that I could not identify.

The docking chamber was small, and I slipped as I stepped out of the submarine. Sarah came over to see if I was alright, but I had only suffered a bruised ego. It was when I pulled myself up that I noticed the steel floor wasn't actually steel at all, but something like a compressed composite plastic. We walked up to a small railing that stuck out in the middle of the wall like a sore thumb when the floor beneath our feet pivoted in one smooth motion, like a secret door I had seen in old-time horror flicks.

We suddenly found ourselves stuck in a very narrow corridor only 10 meters in length, the bottom half of the chamber was lined with an array of tightly set grills. We heard an airless '*Thwump*' of a vacuum tightening pressure seals behind us. Even though the opposite end of the hall had no apparent door, we stepped closer to get a better look.

As Sarah reached the center section, she jumped suddenly and covered her face in panic as several jets of white gas poured out of hidden nozzles in the ceiling and walls. There was no escape in the confined hallway. We coughed as we desperately clung to the sidewall, unable to breathe and gasping for air.

I was to the point of feeling dizzy and losing my balance when the gas finally turned off. Just as quickly, hidden vents sucked out the remaining white fog to leave us dazed and leaning against the walls in anguish.

"What the hell, *cough*, was that?" Sarah forced out of her sore throat as she choked just as a faint buzzer went off from the door behind me. Cautiously, we stepped upon the turnstile plate flooring again in hopes to escape the small chamber. When the door pivoted again, to our disbelief, we found we were no longer in the docking chamber.

"Huh? The whole room must have shifted to another section," Sarah wondered aloud.

"Either that, or another level entirely, like an elevator," I added.

Enormous rough tubes of the gray plasti-cement led us past numerous chambers down several dimly lit hallways. There was a thin film of water droplets lining the walls and floor; we both gave a jump as old air processors kicked in with a whir to draw out the moisture. The air was a bit stale at first, but the vents were swiftly drafting in that same sickly sweet air I had smelled out in the docking bay.

"What is this place, Jim?" Sarah whispered to me as if we were being overheard, and felt a little spooked when I thought about that. I had absolutely no idea where we were.

"I'm not quite sure yet, but look here," I pointed out one hatch door and an unlit keypad at its side, "This is old technology, really old, almost turn of the century style construction."

My hand came away with a streak of dark slime when I touched the surface of the keypad. There was a thin film of some kind of growth lining everything. I took out a glove and wiped away the surface of the door. Beneath it lay the same red painted design, revealing a large B4 plastered on the door. I gave a hopeful three pushes on the '4' button, but nothing happened.

"No luck Sarah, it looks as if we will have to find an open door," I commented.

"I don't get it, why is this place here? I never read any reports or remember anything logged in the history archives about there being a sub-aquatic station on Europa," She exclaimed while wiping away the film of algae, leaving a clean streak across the wall.

"Well, if anything, the Confederation should have had this on its data records," I surmised.

"But it seems abandoned, just like the survey station above. Why would someone go to all the trouble of building this …it certainly must have cost a pretty credit or two," She acknowledged.

"We've got to find some records; most likely they will be in hardcopy," I mentioned with thinning hopes, so we took a look down the passage for any open doors we could find.

Down one section, several gouts of steam were shooting out from leaks in the pipes overhead. As we scurried through the cold mist, the dull drumming of the circulation vents became louder. A room full of huge pistons pumped away at fungus-covered machinery. A few dim lights glowing under the wet slime betrayed the location of a console lying beneath. Wiping it away with a mucked glove, I could see the registered display.

"Look at this Sarah, the ventilation is working *over* efficiency," I pointed to the multicolored screen. The output oxygen levels here were at nearly 80% total atmosphere, which would explain the light euphoria we were experiencing, but why was it cranked up so high? "Well, let's just hope it doesn't climb any higher, since O^2 levels become toxic past 1.6 bars of atmosphere."

I took a closer look at the specs and noticed that the systems ionizers were malfunctioning; I could only suspect that they were either entirely clogged or corroded beyond repair at this point.

The strange film of algae everywhere told me that this place had been abandoned for quite some time, probably just as long as the survey base had been topside. But why a large mining corporation would abandon such an expensive facility of this magnitude was beyond any logic. All the automated gear and machinery that was still functioning could have been recycled at least. This equipment must have been state-of-the-art at the time it was constructed, and would still be worth salvaging even by today's standards. It sure was a mystery.

"Let's just be glad that the life support units are still functioning after all this time," Sarah added.

"Sure, but that sickly stench is starting to worry me. What if it's some sort of infectious bacteria in the air circulation system?" I offered with concern.

"Why not try to repair the ionizers? That would fix the bacterial filters. Who knows …it might clean up all this goo!" Sarah exaggerated while vainly trying to wipe the slime from her hands.

We tried to find access to the adjacent room where I was guessing the electrical systems for the ventilation might be found, but all the doors were firmly sealed. I still didn't get it, how was this facility getting power? The base on the surface operated by solar collectors, but down here there was absolutely no way to get enough

solar energy to light a diode, yet all this machinery
kicked in at full power the minute we walked in the door!
Where was the energy coming from?

I suggested that we split up to find the communications
room, but Sarah wouldn't hear of it. I could imagine she
was a bit spooked, and occasionally the whole station
creaked under the pressure. We stumbled across a few
rooms that looked like medical labs, but it was hard to
tell as everything was painted with the same dark blue
algae. If we were both trapped down here for some time,
I was certain we would never find any edible rations, or
even potable water for that matter.

When the ventilation had started up we had imagined
that the carbon scrubbers had engaged, but we were also
concerned that these might be fully clogged with the
same grime that covered everything else. However, we
noticed that the moisture started to dry up while the air
began to get noticeably warmer as well.

"Look at that, Jim," Sarah pointed out to the corner of
one lab table where various unidentifiable items lay
hidden under the thick muck. What finally caught my
attention was the contrast of color that stood out like a
neon flag. Bundles of bright red waffle-like appendages
were attached there. I could not tell what they were, so I
took a few steps closer to get a better look.

"What is that?" Sarah inquired as she brushed it lightly
with her gloved hand. It suddenly occurred to me that
Sarah's curiosity was the type that leaped before they
bothered to look. I made a fresh mental note to myself
that if we ran across any bright red flashing buttons that
said 'SELF-DESTRUCT' I would make sure to keep her
distracted or tackle her if need be.

A fine powder of spores expelled from the object when

Michel Savage

she touched it, which caused her to cough uncontrollably. I was no biologist, but I knew that couldn't be good. As we stood there, a thin line of red emerged from the algae beside it and began to grow.

"Oh my god, it's blooming!" I announced with shock.

"*cough*, What, *cough*, is?" She sputtered as she choked.

I looked around and noticed that several thin lines began to spread across the room like bloody veins. I quickly grabbed Sarah by the arm.

"We've got to get out of here!" I warned her.

"Why?" Sarah exclaimed, having failed to notice the sudden change in the algae. It took her a short moment to realize something wasn't right as little flowers of red fungus began to ripple up through the dark sheet of slime. We took off at a quick pace down the hall, but the fibrous veins were spreading everywhere, like some giant living being tensing its muscles. We had to get back to the ship, pronto.

"Why is it growing like that?" She choked out.

I shook my head, not knowing the full answer. I was sure if Doc was down here, he would be petting the fungus like a new-found puppy.

"I don't know; it might have been the heaters kicking in, causing it to react." It didn't make much sense to me, but it was the only thing I could think of that might stimulate the sudden growth.

We reached one galley and took a wrong turn, cursing to myself as I realized we had gone the wrong way. We passed through what seemed to be a kitchen facility and immediately noticed a silver steel door that was strangely free of any mildew or growth. As the thin red veins began to spread throughout the room, I pulled Sarah over to the hatch; it appeared to be a freeze locker. I opened the clasp and hurried us inside. Having noticed there was also a handle on the inside, I quickly shut the door to seal us in.

I looked out the small portal window into the room beyond as tiny fins of bright magenta fungus began to sprout everywhere. Since the power had come on recently, it wasn't too cold in the freezer just yet. But it still left me wondering if the water outside of this station must certainly be just as cold, if not colder than the freezer we were now occupying. So why had the algae not grown in here?

"Are we safe from that stuff?" Sarah wondered as she peeked out of the small window.

"I think we are for the moment, the door seal is airtight and probably kept that gunk from getting in here," I mentioned, remembering that these old freezer units had enclosed recirculation air systems for maximum efficiency. Sarah backed away from the door slowly and promptly fell on her rump after she tripped over something she hit with the back of her foot. She suddenly screamed at the top of her lungs, which was very unpleasant in the confined locker.

I turned to see her propped up against the wall. Sitting across from her was a man casting a stone dead stare directly into her eyes only centimeters from her face. I rushed over to help her up, but noticed the man didn't even twitch. His features held the same expression of shock, now staring blankly at the wall where Sarah had sat a moment before.

"Oh god, who is that?" She stuttered with fright.

"I don't know …but he seems quite dead," I responded as I inspected the remains of the poor fellow.

"Did he freeze to death in here?" Sarah whispered to me

as though the corpse was listening.

"That wouldn't make any sense, there's a handle on the door, and the power just cut in. It's weird how he looks almost alive, as though he's only been here a few days at most. If he was one of the original crew, he should have rotted away a long time ago," I mentioned as I dared to edge closer to get a better look, and noticed a thin flaky brown film covering his skin, making him look as though he was peeling from a recent sunburn.

"Hmm, this looks like the same bacteria residue that we found on the bodies at the crash site of that military reconnaissance ship," I pulled on my gloves and tried to pull the corpse out of the corner so I could get a better look at his ID tag. To my utter horror, his whole arm snapped off in my grasp when I tugged. I stood there for a brief moment completely dazed at what had just happened; looking with morbid curiosity at the limb I was holding.

The arm was light and noticeably hollow, as if something had eaten out the entire interior of his body. Only the light rattle of the bones left therein brought me back to my senses, and I dropped the limb immediately in disgust.

"Oh, gross! What the hell happened to him?" Sarah spat with a morbid look on her face as she backed away. I could only shrug my shoulders in confusion.

"It appears as though all his muscles were eaten away," I finally had to draw my eyes away from the hollow cavity of his shoulder. I still couldn't figure out why he looked perfectly whole from the outside, his skin must have solidified during the process of the infection …if that's what it was.

"How long has he been here?" Sarah asked. I took

another peek at the ID badge on his shirt and pulled it off with a sharp tug.

The tag showed the fellow was once a mining engineer, employed by the same company that had placed the survey station topside. The dates on the tag conformed to the construction of the facility topside; but varied by a year or two later, I couldn't remember exactly.

"Why is he here, Jim? I mean, why did he stay behind if they abandoned this base?" Sarah inquired.

That was a damn good question. I took a look at the back of the tag. Along with some numerical data I couldn't decipher, there was some reference to bore drilling. I took a closer look at the body and found a clipboard lying beside him along with several paper files. A lot of the information therein didn't make sense to me, but the graphs showed that they were quarrying a type of ore down here. One of the symbols showed that the product they were mining was some sort of heavy metal …or crystalline in this matter.

"So that crystal is radioactive?" I wondered out-loud.

Sarah came up to peek at the files over my shoulder. "Radioactive? Isn't that bad?"

"Well yes and no …I mean, these charts say they don't crank out enough rads to actually be harmful," Alpha radiation wouldn't be too terribly dangerous to handle, especially if you had robotic drills to do the work, but that led me to think that perhaps the water temperature outside this station would actually be higher than I might have expected.

I began to theorize about the connection of the bacteria that naturally existed in the ice and those one-celled creatures that were floating around outside. Lastly, was this complex running on irradiated power? That would explain how the facility had remained operational after all these years.

"They were mining the crystal that we saw outside, that dark glass that was lining the ocean floor. I think that is what is powering this station," I conceded.

"But why would they purposely mine radioactive ores? That stuff was banned well over a century ago," Sarah debated. I flipped through a few pages and found several output graphs, pointing to the charts.

"This material is well within the safety limits, yet its energy output is far above normal …*hmm*, which doesn't make any sense," I had thought radiation decay was constant, so I didn't understand how this crystal ore could be safe to handle and yet have the energy yield that was shown on these diagrams.

I became aware that the temperature in the freezer was now becoming uncomfortably colder and unmistakably more putrid by the minute. As we were currently in a hermetically sealed room, I realized that we could not possibly stay in here much longer.

Looking outside the tiny window, we saw that the entire room beyond had bloomed into a foul jungle of wavy crimson leaves. The deep rose-colored fins covered everything from floor to ceiling, though a few areas were becoming noticeably darker than others. As we watched, the darker patches spread farther along the room. Ever so slowly, small strips of the fungus withered and died, leaving only a wrinkled flaky crust in its place.

"It's dying off," I whispered to myself as we looked on in wonder. If only Doc were here, he would be able to explain what strange process we were now witnessing. I didn't know why, but perhaps this form of algae was just as sensitive to temperature change as the ice itself was above. This was one strange moon.

When enough of the fungus had shriveled, I grabbed Sarah so we could escape the freezer that was becoming increasingly unlivable by the second. The dead withered fins crunched beneath our feet, leaving a wake of the noxious powder floating in the air behind us. We knew we couldn't stop moving, or we would succumb to the fine cloud of spores we had kicked up.

Sarah pointed out the doorway we had entered from, and the pivoting door took us back to the confined hall once again, which I had expected was some sort of pressurization room. There was no choking gas sprayed this time, but I did notice a slight hum of movement in the walls. After it ceased, we stepped onto the pivoting floor once again and were gratefully returned back to the docking bay, but something was terribly wrong.

We stood there with our mouths open in utter shock... the mini-sub was gone!

Standoff

The situation was tense. Roller thought he had done a decent job of keeping his cool thus far, despite the circumstances but Sarge's presence had effectively thrown a wrench into the works and damned their plan all to hell. He couldn't even begin to fathom the twisted lies Sarge might have been feeding to Turvel and his minions, but it was clear he had already started manipulating their desperate situation to his own advantage.

Sarge was certainly a master at deceit; he had fooled all of his crew until the last moment when he had shown his hand. Even though Roller was holding the gun, he knew he would have to choose his words wisely to gain back Turvel's trust. Blasting Sarge on the spot might not accomplish that too effectively. The Sergeant was unarmed and stood there casually as if giving them all a dramatic pause to ponder. This caused Roller to stall for a moment while he tried to think of what to do next.

As Roller struggled to grasp the initiative, Sarge casually strolled over past Turvel and suddenly grabbed the Professor around the neck, putting him into a solid headlock. In the same swift motion, Turvel's sonic pistol was snatched from his belt and into Sarge's hand as he pressed the muzzle against the old man's frazzled head.

The armed guards had no time to react to the officer's trained reflexes, and this situation turned the tables against Roller's favor. Everyone in the room flinched simultaneously. Even Turvel seemed to have paused at this sudden turn of events.

"Well my friend," Sarge grinned as he nodded to Roller, "I think you best put that toy gun down before you hurt someone, or else your companion here gets scrambled brains for breakfast!" The way Sarge stated this so mildly made it a chilling thought.

Roller didn't know how to react – should he put the rifle down and face either getting killed on the spot or start blasting away, despite that the poor Prof was in the way? The Professor's desperate eyes made the decision for him.   There was no other way to save his life at the moment.   The red guards watched him tensely as he unstrapped the assault rifle from his shoulder and slowly laid it on the floor. With a cold scowl of defeat, Roller raised his hands above his head hesitantly.

Sarge let the old man go with a shove and handed the pistol back over to Turvel, who eyed him warily for the brief moment it took him to grasp the handgun, as if he was resizing him on the spot. It was apparent Turvel wasn't comfortable with someone that had unarmed him so effortlessly in front of his men, but the returning of his weapon had helped him save face, making it almost look like the whole incident was planned; which, of course, was far from the truth. The Prof huddled in the corner as he rubbed his neck, gasping for air.

"Oh, don't look so glum, soldier," Sarge mocked, as the red guards began to bind Roller's hands behind his back. "You and I should have a nice long chat about where the rest of your team is, and how you were planning to deceive everyone into sparking a rebellion."

At that, Turvel ordered his men to hold Roller in a bolted cargo room at the rear of the ruined ship. The Prof could only look on speechlessly while keeping a respectable distance from Cross. He had to try to find a way to get a word in with Turvel, to convince him that Roller was telling the truth, but there was no way to do that with this mercenary hovering around him. For the moment, he would have to bide his time, which he had taken as a commodity for so long in the past; but now, time was quickly running out for them all.

Roller sat in the dark, spitting out blood from his split lip one of the guards decided to lavish him with a swift kick while no one was watching. He was now beginning to regret ever trying to save these wretches; though deep down, he knew the truth was that there were actually a sizable number of inmates incarcerated here who were innocent of any legitimate charges, or who were framed for petty crimes and did not deserve their imprisonment upon this ice moon.

The Confederation would pay for all of this if they got caught, but taking out Sarge was a personal matter now. At that moment, something clicked in Roller and his stubborn ethics bent for the sweet taste of revenge. The cold look in his hard eyes seemed to burn away the darkness. The door swung open to his holding cell and the sergeant's shadow fell across the bound soldier.

"Well, my friend, you look comfortable," Sarge uttered with a chuckle. Roller was strapped with his hands tied behind his back to a loose pipe, while he struggled on his knees to keep himself upright. He gave no response except for a hostile glare of hatred.

"Not too happy to see me alive, eh, old pal?" He continued to mock, "No thanks to that petty engineer of yours," Sarge stated while gingerly touching the fresh jagged scar along his neck, "I almost suffocated to death. But in a strange way, another unfortunate accident saved me so that I could have the chance to savor this priceless moment," he spat out those last words with detest.

Roller didn't quite understand what he was getting at, as Jim had never explained about the broken seals to the cockpit of the transport ship, but he did wonder why the hell Sarge would bother not to escape off-planet when he had the chance.   Sarge's unpredictable mood changed like the direction of the wind as he pointed to his scar.

"I think I'll give that little bastard a matching souvenir just like this one." he smiled, "It seems like the one thing I failed to do on my mission actually ended up saving my ass. I guess two wrongs do make a right! *Hah ha, ha*," he laughed unsteadily. Roller was still confused as to what Sarge was referring to.

"I don't get it, Sarge. You got away clean, why come back?" Roller grumbled with genuine interest.

"I had just reached orbit when all the systems began to run through their diagnostic program as that damn Sentinel scanned my ship. *Hmph*, well, I guess those damn satellites were better shielded than we had thought," he smirked, "The transport kicked into self-destruct mode, but of course, our Tech was kind enough to have disabled that for us. But when I got hit with that gamma-ray burst from the Sentry, the ship's systems went off-line just the same. There is hardly any atmosphere on this damn snowball to glide on; my forced landing wasn't too pleasant ...as you can see," Sarge made sure Roller was looking at him as he opened up his shirt to show the long scar running from his neck, far down along his torso. It was a horrid wound, and Roller wondered how he had survived it.

It was the native bacteria, of course, which was especially effective in healing the epidermal layer. By sheer chance, he had crash-landed on a fault in the ice where a thick vein of bacteria had breached the surface. After crawling his way out of the wreckage, Sarge had struggled to pack his wound with ice to dull the pain, unknowingly doing the one thing that could save him as he lay dying, numb with shock and bleeding to death. In the several days that passed, his injury healed at an accelerated rate.

Then the Raiders found him, and he befriended them with a fake name and a few well-placed lies to convince them that he was a prisoner who had been the only survivor of a transport malfunction. The busted drone ship helped to credit his story; there wasn't much left of the shuttle to examine closely as it was anyways.

When he met Turvel, he quickly escalated his story to meet his own ends. Now he had decent control of the situation at hand, except for the fact that a fleet of Confederation ships would be running into a fully functioning Sentry armament, which might cause a few unexpected problems for his rescue off this miserable planet. His interstellar communicator had burned out when he was struck down by the satellite and he had to find another source of communication to radio them before the armada arrived. Roller and his expendable crewmates might prove to be the answer to that little problem, he realized.

Sarge stood there sneering at the bound soldier, thinking of something cocky to say, or perhaps how he could press more information out of him. A shadow fell lightly across his back; Sarge was usually quick to such movements, but he was distracted while gloating over his prisoner. He turned his head slowly to look over his shoulder just as a heavy steel bar cracked across his head with a sickening metallic '*Thunk*'.

Sarge dropped to the ground like a stone. The silhouette replacing him was that of the shaking Professor, holding a rather large pipe. Roller glanced down at the lump of flesh that was Sarge lying sprawled across the floor and back up to the Prof, who was still stunned that he had managed to get the drop on Sarge.

"My hero..." Roller tried to smile, but winced from the nasty cut on his lip. The Professor let the thick pipe drop to the floor with a dull clang, "Ah... a little help here, please," Roller added. The Prof immediately scurried over to untie him.

"We've gotta get out of here quick, young man. Turvel seemed a bit upset about that little incident in front of his men. They're all busy right now prepping the wind-sails to scout the crash site of that Confederation ship. I don't want to be around when they find you aren't here to give them directions."

Roller grunted in pain from the few bruises he had suffered from the guards but managed to follow the old man out a back passage. Nightfall would be coming soon and the Raider sleds would be prepared to depart on their expedition. They had to get to their rover and back to the survey base. If what Sarge had said was true, then the Sentry would also shoot down the mining shuttle that was on its way to rescue them. He had to warn them!

They slipped past a room full of Turvel's guards and outside the building through a forgotten side hatch that the Prof had managed to pry open. Roller was changing his mind about this old kook, and had to give him some credit for the effort he had put in for saving his ass. Slipping out from the complex to the outer rim was the tricky part, as there was a lot of open space to cover across the courtyard and into the shadows of the shanty buildings beyond.

Several of the Raiders were busy prepping the sails and adjusting their skids for nightfall when the ice froze over in the few hours to come. Their luck ran out when they scurried across the yard and leaned against a shoddily constructed wall of steel and pipes, all of which came tumbling down around them with enough noise to draw the attention of everyone in sight. Roller gritted his teeth as all the siding and pipes fell apart and clanged together with no way of stopping it.

The Professor's eyes widened, "They see us, run!"

Roller took a quick glance over to the Raider ships and saw that all heads had turned towards them. He took a leap between the shacks as shouts arose from behind him. All he could do was follow the old man and try to ignore the pain from his bruised ribs. They had a good fifty meters on their pursuers, but the steep rim of the outer hill was still in front of them. The Prof scrambled up on all fours, while Roller attempted to follow in suit. One of his cracked ribs made him pause, and a sharp pain lanced through his back. He reached around blindly with his left hand to find a thin steel spike; one of those bastards armed with a makeshift crossbow had managed to find their mark.

He ripped out the bolt and flung it aside, and his adrenaline kicked in. Roller scrambled up over the hill and tumbled down the other side. The Professor saw the thin trail of blood and ran back over to help the soldier along. The Raiders were gaining fast, but as they turned the slope to another snowdrift they found the rover. Roller took a brief moment to slump on the side of the vehicle, taking in a deep cold breath. The Prof was eyeing him anxiously, "Get this thing started!" He nearly screamed.

Roller was beginning to feel the effects of his wounds, the sharp searing pain and a noticeable loss of motor function in his limbs. He felt as if he was going to black out at any moment, but knew that would be the end of him and the Professor if he did. Roller quickly punched in the code to activate the rover with one hand, as he unlatched a pulse rifle with the other. The gun unhooked from the inside rim of the vehicle's interior. It was an older series of the sonic weapons, with a thick stout barrel and hefty resonance chamber. It bore a roughly etched image of a skull and crossbones upon its shaft that he had scratched there during a random moment of boredom a few days back.

The Raiders came scurrying around the corner of the hillside just as he lifted the big gun up over the lip of the vehicle and pointed it in their direction. Some of the guards hesitated, while others dove for cover. Roller really wasn't aiming to kill anyone, but he also wasn't feeling in much of a generous mood at the moment either. The outmoded gun had one setting. It shot a ball of compressed sound waves at the group of Raiders, just hitting the ground at the foot of the foremost guard.

The frost around them exploded with a dull thunderclap that left a sizable crater in the snow. Two of the convicts got caught in the radius of the blast. Roller didn't know if it had killed them, but they certainly weren't moving. He tried to pull himself into the rover, but could only manage to tumble into the cargo area in the back.

The Prof leapt into the driver's seat and fiddled with the gears nervously. Roller didn't know what the old man was trying to do as the vehicle lurched back and forth with a grinding of gears; he heard the Professor swear frequently while doing so.   He tried to get into the driver's seat but just couldn't manage to find the strength to even peek over the lip of the vehicle to see how close Turvel's red guards were closing in.

It was then that he passed out... and he knew the Prof certainly didn't know how to drive their land rover.   It was not a pleasant thought to go under with.

Conspiracy

It was hopeless, how the hell did the damn submarine disappear on us? We were stuck, and the thought of returning to that morbidly cold freezer started to seem marginally attractive compared to this claustrophobic docking port.

"We have to go back in," was all I could manage to say.

"But…" Sarah mumbled with a defeated pout pausing on her lips. I think she realized we really had no other choice at the moment.

We cycled through the pressure door, fully expecting the gas to activate once again, but were relieved to find that the system was smart enough to realize that no new ships had docked. We both secretly held our breath as the hallway door cycled open, but the spores we feared inhaling had been sucked up through the ventilation. Several breaking stalks popped out a cloud of spores that were quickly whisked away through the nearest vent, though the stubborn sickly-sweet tinge permeating the air still remained.

Rotting fungus crunched under our heavy boots as we explored the rest of the facility. I finally found a data port that led us to the Head Director's quarters. Several of the lifts refused to function, so we had to make use of the constrictive circular stairwells that littered the upper levels.

The director's chamber was a disastrous mess, as if someone had done a thorough and indiscriminate search of the entire room. There were plastic data sheets strewn everywhere about the floor, I only found a few with any bits of worthy information.

"It looks as if they were solely mining that crystal ore at this site, and had a staff of over 400 engineers at this station," I whistled with surprise. It made sense, this facility was pretty big, but from my previous studies, only a dozen scientists were on crew for the surface base. Was, in fact, most of the work being done here under the ice, and why had it been kept a secret all these years?

"I don't get it Jim; I covered all the operations files intensively. There was absolutely no mention of an actual mining facility operating on Europa," Sarah conceded. I paused to scratch my head, only to stop to think I should give the Doc a stout punch in the shoulder for cursing me with that habit.

"What we have here, Sarah, is a real puzzle," I paused for thought as I shuffled through the files, "This black crystal ore lining the ocean floor serves as an efficient power source, one that would definitely be of value back home, so why stop mining it? Furthermore, why haven't any samples of this particular element even reached Earth? Besides, it doesn't take much intelligence to figure out that this fungus…" I motioned to the flaky crust lining the room, "efficiently produces oxygen, so the question is; why were both of these extremely valuable resources left abandoned?"

Sarah squirmed for a moment, as if she was in deep thought. Which I knew was not very likely, as I smirked to myself.

"Well, you saw how this fungus responds to slight temperature changes. Perhaps it reacts dangerously in artificial environments," she offered.

So I stood corrected. She did have a valid point, but I still didn't fully buy that explanation. Spacesuits were a dime-credit a dozen, so surely a crew fitted with modern hazard suits could easily keep this highly expensive facility operational. It had been done on many other unfriendly environments such as large meteors and gas planets. Compared to those climates, this would have been a piece of cake to control. No, something more sinister was at the root of all of this.

Within the mess littering the Directors room, I came across a data cube tucked away at the back drawer of his desk. It was labeled in bold letters as "family photos" but what caught my attention was the technical data that was coded underneath the label. Only another engineer would have noticed that the configuration of the periodic table had been oddly rearranged, and that it was secretly marked as a vital file. The non-compatible elements symbols Ru, Cr, Mg, Fe, Hn, and Mt, were strategically placed to spell out the word; URGENT.

I wiped off the grit from the digital cube and cleaned off the screen from the data port in his room. Sarah helped to get the thing running; static cut in at first after we plopped in the cube, but the image came through after a few seconds. We certainly didn't like what we saw. A red-bearded man in a dark green jumpsuit spoke nervously from the screen.

"This is Director Hamilton of the Europa project," he licked his dry lips as his eyes darted away for a nervous moment; "our station has been overrun by troops of Confederate police who are gunning down our men in cold blood. Reports are coming in that they are dumping the bodies out of the airlock and into the ocean. We have no weapons to effectively defend ourselves. They came to us only hours ago under false pretenses, then blocked off the exits to the submarine ports. There is no escape for us!" He stammered while a loud banging could be heard in the background, "We have discovered a highly efficient power source here deep within the ocean of this moon, and the ice here naturally produces oxygen at a higher proficiency than our own native Terran plants. These two elements could greatly escalate our methods of establishing off-world colonies, but we recently uncovered evidence that the Confederation has been secretly blockading and seizing all our transports back to Earth and scrambling our communications in an attempt to sabotage our discoveries here on Europa. We were going to expose the corruption of the military forces as it appears they have been intentionally undermining every effort of the civilian and private sector colonists from ever leaving Earth."

In the background the pounding became louder, most likely what we were hearing was the discharge of old-style firearms. The Director looked saddened, defeated, and deathly fatigued, "It seems our arrogant threat to uncover their plot against the citizens of Earth has been our death warrant. We have no way to escape from this submerged facility. If anyone finds this message in time, the last of us will try to hide in the drilling tunnels for as long as we can. Our best chance, our *only* chance is to evade them within the labyrinth of the mines."

The recording was quickly terminated after that last line. After the transmission log faded to black, a deep sickening feeling wrenched my gut, wondering just how long those few survivors must have lingered in the dark tunnels, cringing in fear at every suspicious noise, and eventually starving to death in the darkness.

Their distress call was finally received ...a century too late. I popped out the data cube and held it tight in my sweating palm... was this also going to be our fate? Sarah's face went pale with worry as the console screen powered down.

  It all made sense now. Back when the invention of light drive was in its infancy and being installed in new starships, the heads of the power-hungry military did whatever they could to keep all their taxpaying citizens anchored on Earth. I could imagine how worried they became when a private civilian corporation found both an economically available and pliable form of fission material, plus a hyper-oxygen creating bacteria to boot. These particular elements would have been very valuable to off-world terraformers, which would only help to increase their numbers as pioneers and they're families migrated from Earth to colonize the stars. This would have left the Confederation to tightening their belts, and the greedy little generals would certainly have frowned upon that!

  They surely would have had the personnel on hand to do their dirty deeds and could orchestrate the cover-up with a few well-placed bribes to a handful of unethical officers they could easily reassign as needed for the task. It was not uncommon to have civilians go missing on dangerous interplanetary projects. Most everything off-planet was usually handled under the jurisdiction of the watchful eye of the Confederation, whom the public funded and trusted to oversee their safety. Oh, how they were duped.

  Since most citizens had left earth for interstellar destinations decades ago, the J6 project had become just a little 'too' effective at curbing crime, so they had started condemning minor offenders. They had even stooped to the point of framing certain individuals just to keep the crime statistics up so that the numbers would justify their budget. What a bunch of bastards!

"What do we do now Jim?" Sarah asked timidly.

"Let's search the facility for a way to contact the surface base; they must have had some sort of system for internal communications to the facility up top." Though I feared that any installed transmitters must have been sabotaged long ago by the military troops during their raid, but it still wouldn't hurt to take a look.

"All those people - just murdered..." She whispered, the words catching in her throat. It was no wonder that the Confederation wanted to get to J6 first; they had a lot of dirty laundry they had to clean up along with erasing all of the surviving inmate's topside. There was nothing we could do to help the situation from down here. We might even survive a few days, or possibly a few weeks or so, considering if we had been affected by the local microbes ingested through the native water supply, but we had to eat solid food sometime.

We both turned as something down the corridor creaked, then a harsh slamming of steel caught our immediate attention. Sarah flashed a worried look to me, had the Troopers landed and decided to sweep this facility for the sake of efficiency? All sorts of wild and unpleasant thoughts ran through my head. They were most likely down here to plant explosives to destroy the station entirely, that way it couldn't be picked up by any modern orbital scanners. I found a loose stick of plastic furniture to use as a weapon, realizing it was a bit too light to be of any use against a fully armored trooper, I grabbed Sarah's arm and bolted down the hall.

"We have to hide," I cautioned.

"But, where?" Sarah blurted innocently, "Military issue

thermal scanners will pick us up in a nanosecond," she stated between breaths as we jogged down the corridor.

"Well, I'm not going down without a fight!" I affirmed coldly as we slipped into a pump room, hoping that its heavy electromagnetic pulse might somehow help to mask our presence from their scanners. To my satisfaction, I found a few tools there and settled my grip on a hefty metal bar with an oddly ribbed hook that performed some function I could only guess at. Sarah crouched on the other side of the door and grabbed a small bolt cutter as a hand weapon. I put my finger to my lips to gesture her to be silent as we began to hear several heavy footsteps coming down the hall beyond the doorway.

It was hard to tell how many there were as the dried fungus crunched underneath their boots. But perhaps if I could knock one out with a lucky blow and grab his gun, then at least we would have a fighting chance; a sorry-ass chance, but one none the least.

I started to sweat and tightened my grip of the metal bar as I heard a few more doors cycle open and their footsteps were coming closer. Obviously, they were searching each of the rooms thoroughly. Sarah nervously fingered her sharp bolt cutter as the steps came nearer and I prepared to swing my bar at head height with all my strength. It would probably take that to knock down a Confederate trooper wearing a standard armored helmet, and I knew I would only get one chance.

I tried to time it right, hoping I wouldn't screw it up by aiming too high. The soldier took one step into the doorway and I swung with all my might as soon as I saw his shadow cross the entrance. He must have seen Sarah first, because out of the corner of my eye I noticed a look of stark surprise flash across her face.

"No, Jim, wait!" Sarah yelled as she flung her hands up.

Too late; the trooper was agile for being in full armor, for he ducked under my swing just as it would have connected, and the metal bar clanged against the plasti-steel door frame. I swung far too hard, as the shock of the impact jolted my wrist and knocked the bar out of my grasp. Crap, that really hurt! I cradled my injured hands just as I saw the would-be trooper glance quickly in my direction, though oddly, he wasn't wearing a helmet. In fact, it wasn't a military soldier at all ...it was Voc!

I was too startled to react in the split second it took for the metal bar to bounce out of my hands and deflect off the side of his skull before it clanged to the floor. Voc almost collapsed as he grabbed for his wounded head, I bent down to help him when I looked up to see Rook's cold stare meet mine, the shiny metal tube of a pulse gun was aimed straight between my eyes. My mouth fell open at that moment and I turned visibly pale.

She immediately brought the gun back up as soon as she recognized me. I can only imagine how many milliseconds I had been away from getting my brains scrambled. Sarah attempted to help Voc get to his feet.

"How did you guys get down here?" Sarah inquired, the answer was obvious though. Rook holstered her gun and turned to help me with my aching wrists.

"We, *ugh*, took some sort of mini-submersible down here," Voc blurted out in obvious pain. Rook just shot a look into my eyes, I could tell there was a flash of relief showing in her face.

"We were looking for you two, but that damn robot was blocking the doorway to the drilling room. It took a while to get that thing out of the way," Rook mentioned.

"And we found that hole under the ice," Voc added, "I fiddled around with a few of the controls, and apparently hit some sort of button that retracted the submersible that brought us down here."

Hmm, a recall switch; so that's why the manta sub disappeared on us. The question was, did the ship depart back for the surface once it dropped their two friends off and leave us all stranded here? Voc must have been reading my mind as he interpreted the worried look on my face.

"We left Dr. Brendan topside with instructions to watch the monitors, the sub should still be in dock. By the way... what is this place?" Voc inquired.

"Sorry about the bump on the head, Voc," I grumbled apologetically, "Follow me; there's something you two have got to see."

We walked back down the hallway, the dead fungus crunching under our feet as little wisps of spores were whisked away through the vents behind us. Doc would have certainly gone wild down here, collecting samples of everything in sight, but he was one of our only contacts topside to ensure our safe return.

"This is an old quarry; they were mining radioactive ore here under the ice. From what we saw from the outside, the moon's core seems to be made of the stuff," I yielded.

"Radioactive?" Voc jolted out.

"Don't worry, it's very low-level stuff, and we are well protected here," I added as we made our way back to the director's chamber, "The Confederation shut this place down for personal reasons," I spat out as I pulled the data cube out of my pocket and into the slot in front of the screen.

Both the technicians watched the video with interest,

but not a hint of disbelief crossed their faces. After what we've been through these past few days, nothing dirty about the Confederation could shock us anymore.

After the log terminated, I popped the data cube back out and dropped it into my pocket, "This," I added as I patted my pocket, "is proof enough to get the civilian forums back on earth to charge the Confederation with anti-trust crimes and initiate a full investigation."

"Boldly stated," Rook broke in, "but we still have to get off this snowball first."

Oh right, one thing at a time. We had to get topside immediately and send this data to the mining facility on Mars. They would make sure this information went public, but we still had the task of fending off the incoming squadrons and sneak our way onto the rescue ship, and then pray that we weren't shot down by an armada of Confederation battle cruisers as we left the planet. Facing all that, maybe staying down here wasn't such a bad idea after all.

"The rescue ship will be here in less than 12 hours, I'm just surprised the military hasn't arrived already," Voc put in. I had assumed that they had already stationed a vessel near Ganymede, but I could have been wrong.

"They might have already touched down on the far side of the planet and are busy rounding up the inmates for execution while they work their way to this side of the hemisphere," Sarah added sarcastically, but her tone changed to the seriousness of her statement.

"No, I don't think so," Voc replied. Rook filled in the rest of his sentence.

"We've been monitoring all frequencies; but nothing came up over the surface static, it almost seems like there's been a blackout of communications, if anything,"

She added with an afterthought.

"Well, we have to get back to the Com room at the Survey Base as soon as possible and zap out this information on the transmitter," I urged.

All four of us nodded in agreement and we headed directly for the docking chamber. I was quite relieved to find the sub was still there, but my stress was only replaced with worry if we were all going to be able to fit into the 2-person cockpit. None of us truly wanted to stay behind, as there seemed to be no way to recall the ship from the underwater port, so all four of us crammed into the wide seat.

"I sure hope this thing spurts out enough air to keep all of us breathing," Voc offered with a nervous grin as he hit a series of orange buttons that flashed simultaneously. My one worry was wondering if this thing could cart us all back to the surface, considering it was now carrying twice the weight. All the amber lights turned green one by one, and the shield cycled shut over us.

After a few tense moments, the cell filled with water, and the docking doors behind us opened. The ship slowly backed out of the port, and we tried to get comfortable as possible crowding each other in the small cockpit. Voc punched a few more buttons as his hands wavered over the console as though he wasn't exactly sure what he was doing. To my horror, he reached under the right console screen and pulled out a fistful of wires and began disconnecting their couplings, seemingly at random.

"How were you able to make sense of all this?" I questioned with a slight squeak in my voice as I nervously watched him popping wires loose in sequence. The sub sped on back up the way we came, however this time the upper crust of ice was noticeably darker. He answered me without taking his attention away from his immediate task.

"Interplanetary engineers are a strange lot." He added with a smirk, "All these icons on the screen and control buttons refer to basic functions, almost like using pictures instead of words. Actually, it's quite ingenious in its own way. It was just their technique to make operating all of their equipment basically 'idiot-proof' so to speak," he turned for just a second to look at me. It was then that I noticed he was only dismantling the white wires on the umbilical he was holding.

"The only problem with that system though is that it isn't exactly universal; you pretty much have to be an engineer to understand the basic symbols, pretty much everyone else would be shit out of luck." Well, that made sense, considering the old fashioned systems they were using during that era.

"So, how did you know how to read these symbols?" I inquired. Voc just smiled as he finished reconnecting all the white wires back together.

"Well, I don't exactly; I was just making an educated guess ...but I didn't want to worry you," he smiled. That comment almost made me faint. The two women let out a silent gasp as all our heads turned to him in dismay.

"Actually, most of the controls for this sub are automated from the lab on the surface. There are several transmitter beacons along the route. As you can see, they show up on the screen, but I presume the power supply for their strobes has long since burned out, but they still reflect the relay coordinates efficiently. I made sure the program was running for a return trip and instructed Doc to hit a few switches when I signaled him through the vital systems," he assured us.

"But, um, what are you doing there?" Sarah dared to ask as she pointed at the jumble of wires.

"Just rerouting some of the primary systems… so that in the event we have an emergency and need this sub to get back down to that aquatic station, it won't be able to be automatically recalled back to the surface unless we allow it to by reconnecting it manually."

Oh, well I guess I should put more faith in Voc and his background in electronic systems. Considering how old this hardware was, it was probably a cakewalk for him to take this thing apart. For a moment there, I thought he was screwing with our guidance system and wanted to take this thing for a joyride. Then, of course, finding that one tiny vent hole in this vast ceiling of ice would be nearly impossible.

Our ship sped through the clouds of amoeba and up to the drilled cavity in the ice we had emerged from. This trip was far less turbulent than our descent, and the spotlights from our sub lit up the tunnel of ice with a soft glow as we glided towards the surface. The vid-screen on the console displayed our position as we approached sea level. However, we were still far from the surface of the icecap.

We bobbed there in the dark tunnel for several minutes as we watched a long rod snake it's way down from the pinpoint of light far above. With a disturbing jolt, the arm found its connection point and our little ship was drawn up through the rest of the tunnel at an alarming rate. The sides of the sub grazed the walls of the tunnel more than a few times during our ascent, which caused the ship to spin uncontrollably. We held onto each other nervously and let out a sigh of relief when we finally breached the lip of the vent and an automated rail settled the ship back into dry dock.

We saw Doc standing by the doorway, respectively clear of all the spinning machinery until our shield cycled back to let us out of the cockpit. We all pretty much jumped out of that little submarine, for fear that the carnival ride might start all over again.

"Are you guys alright?" Doc inquired cautiously, as we were obviously a bit shaken from our excursion through the tunnel. Rook almost looked like she was going to be sick. The one good thing was the cold air up here didn't have that nauseatingly sweet stench to it that saturated the aquatic station below.

Charlie the robot sat patiently in the far back hall, his one green eye was still glowing dimly, completely unconcerned with our plight.

"Yeah, thanks Doc, we owe you one," I tried to smile, but my stomach was still churning from the ride up, and I was trying to pop my ears as I shook my head from the drastic change in altitude we experienced. I saw Sarah stumble over the thick wires lining the floor as she headed for the door.

"Let's get to the communications room, shall we," I motioned towards the exit as we all unceremoniously scrambled for the door.

Using the remote, I had to order the bot to clear the back doorway. The clunky old robot obeyed without complaint. We rushed through the bay area and found Min Li sitting back with a pair of headphones on and his legs kicked up on the console. He nearly fell out of his chair as we startled him when our group barreled into the communications room.

"Whoa …hey, where have you guys been?" He asked.

"Have you heard back from Roller yet?" Rook countered impatiently while ignoring his question.

"Uh, no... I've been monitoring all the frequencies since you left, but there's been nothing but empty static," Min answered with a shrug of his shoulders. Hmm, that also meant that the Troopers hadn't landed yet. But of course, they might have been using some sort of military sub-frequency for their communications on this covert operation, so anything was possible.

"We should check in on Roller and the Professor, it seems to me like they're a bit overdue," Rook advised. She pulled Min out of his seat and plopped down without pause, and began adjusting the scanners. She didn't call for him on the mike, but whatever she did; it didn't take long to get an answer.

"It appears that his radio is turned off, I'm not getting any response signal, there's no way to reach him until he activates it," she replied without turning back to face us.

At that moment, I heard Charlie lurch into action down the hall. As I hustled into the main dome, the bot clanked its way directly towards the bay doors. Something inside of its housing was whirring softly. I reached around to pop open the robot's access panel to take a look at the readout. It had picked up movement outside, something was approaching the Base.

I closed the panel and spoke into Charlie's remote, ordering the huge metal contraption to hide in the shadows at the corner of the bay doors. Positioned there, the bot effectively blended into the mess of pipes, wires, and crane machinery. Sarah ventured to take a peek up top, but I pulled her back inside. It was dark out now, so spotting trooper ships against the stars would be a bit difficult.

I cautiously crept up the snow tunnel to the surface and took a look around. A flash of light over a distant hill caused me to duck suddenly back down the hole, but I dared another peek. Nothing ...then another distant flash of light through the fog betrayed that something was heading our way. Careening up over a low hill and seemingly out of control, I could see the headlights of our land rover. Why the hell was Roller driving so recklessly?

I called back down to my crew who were anxiously waiting at the bay doors. Min and Voc scrambled up first, while the women stayed behind. The vehicle was coming at high speed, and I froze once it turned and caught me dead center in its glaring headlights. The problem with electric motors is that they are almost noiseless and you can't hear them over-revving. So there I stood in the harsh wind as the vehicle came barreling along in the cold silence, blinding me in its headlights until something began to click in my head that the rover wasn't going to stop!

Being on top of the situation, Voc grabbed me by the collar and pulled me down as Min dove the other way. The rover's tires skidded along the ice and slammed violently into the side of the dome, directly where all three of us had been standing just a split second before. Apparently, the vehicle was still on its 4-wheel drive mode, but it had already turned nightfall and the surface had long since frozen over. If the rover had its skis on, I'm pretty sure it would have ramped right up over the dome at that speed.

Something began burning in the engine as the rover lay half propped up upon the dome. A few internal gears could be heard becoming increasingly agitated with the sudden halt of their external counterparts. The Prof was laying half out of the driver's seat, looking quite dazed. Roller, on the other hand, nearly flopped out of the back before we rushed over to catch him.

"Uh... *heh*, um, sorry about that," the Prof babbled.

"What happened?" Min asked urgently as he pulled his bloodied hand away from the soldiers back.

"Well, perhaps we should get him inside first," the old man mumbled out, slightly shaken.

Min Li nodded his approval at the Professor while he and I got under one arm each and helped Roller down through the bay doors and into the lab. Sarah cleared off a table, while our medic went to work on him. The Prof hobbled over and plopped down into one of the nearby chairs.

"Sorry about wrecking your transport," he apologized through short breaths. I went over to the Professor while Sarah offered him a canteen of water.

"Are you alright there, Professor?" I asked, and he gave a curt wave of approval, "You came in pretty hot up there and nearly ran us down." It was hard to read the old man, but he gave a pretty pitiful look of embarrassment.

"I don't have a clue how to drive that thing, but we didn't have much of a choice at the time," he gestured over to Roller, who was not very responsive to anything at the moment.

"I take it Turvel didn't welcome his friendly advice," Min added in from behind them while he was busy examining Roller's wound. Doc took out a hypo from his bag and gave him a shot to keep him under. Rook gave the doctors a worried look.

"How serious is it?" she asked with a tone of concern.

"Don't know yet, it doesn't look like a high-velocity

puncture, and a sonic weapon wouldn't have made this kind of wound. What was he hit with?" Min asked as he turned to the Prof.

"I can't say ...I didn't see. It was those damn Raiders that got him. It could have been a spear or a knife," he responded as he shrugged his shoulders. The Professor pointed over to one of his cabinets full of experimental cultures and gestured to Min, "After you clean the wound, you should apply the bacteria marked 'A-47', it's one of the purified forms." Having gone over those cultures before with the Prof, Min knew what he was talking about and nodded in agreement.

"What happened out there, Professor?" Sarah finally asked, and the rest of us in the room jointly turned our attention back to the old man as he nursed the canteen of water. One of his unexpected and always out of place chuckles escaped his lips, and then his face went serious.

"Well things kind of got out of hand when this stranger showed up and got a little too buddy-buddy with ole' Turvel," he answered. That got us all wondering.

"A stranger ...what are you talking about?" I returned. The old man just shrugged his shoulders.

"Some lout I've never seen before. He was ugly and bald, with a stout face, and kinda muscular too. I think I heard Turvel call him Cross, but Roller seemed to know him. He said his name once, sumth'in like; *Sarge*?" He shrugged as if that was supposed to mean something. It sure as hell did! All of us in the room shared a startled, hollow stare. Why would Sarge come back?

Assault

I had thought those faulty seals on the transport ship would have done Sarge in for good. Perhaps he caught slight suspicion of that before he left the atmosphere and turned back to finish us off. The Confederation troops would be landing at any moment, so he had plenty of back-up on the way. Still, the part about him getting friendly with the natives on this penal colony just didn't sit right. Something smelled funny about all this.

"Well, we still have to get that message out on broadband about what we found under the ice. Rook, come help me get that call channel back online," Voc motioned to the pale siren.

Rook flicked back her white hair and gave me a questionable look right before she tromped off to the communications room. I didn't know if Sarah had noticed that, but she didn't say anything for the moment. Doc washed his bloodied hands off with a wet cloth after he finished patching up Roller, whose muscle-bound form lay strewn across the lab table.

"He should be fine, with a bit of rest; but we can't move him," Doc mentioned with a slight tilt of his head towards his patient.

We could only hope that our rescue ship would get here before the military squadrons showed up to finalize their plans. Voc called us back to the communications console where we tried to contact the mining ship that was on its way. We got nothing but waves of static.

"Communications have gone dark," Rook stated coldly, "the damaged antenna can't get through a whole planet of ice. We need a line of sight to make contact again, there's nothing we can do until sunrise." Everyone let out a silent moan. The Troopers would definitely be here long before we made contact with our rescue ship or could possibly send any information out by open wave towards Earth.

I certainly didn't think we would have the luxury of another 20 plus hours of peace and quiet until the moon completed its rotation. There were bloodthirsty convicts roaming the surface at night and a well-armed militia dropping in on us from above.

"So that's it, we're screwed until the mining ship gets here?" Min asked with overbearing concern.

"By my estimates," Voc put in while scribbling on a digital chart, "it's going to be a close one. Our rescue ship and the Confederation squadrons will likely arrive in orbit within the same hour. That is, if they didn't have any military cruisers already stationed closer, and if my calculations of their flight speed are correct, and other variances of course…" He mumbled on.

"Well, let's just hope," Sarah cut him off. Hearing Voc babble on sometimes was a little much.

"How soon do you think Voc?" I tried to inquire, realizing I might have just sabotaged Sarah's efforts to shut him up. Luckily, he cut straight to the point with his answer.

"Two hours …three tops," he replied with a shrug.

Suddenly, something in my coat beeped. I groped around in the various pockets inside my jacket until I found the robot's remote. Why the hell did that thing go off? It was the first time it had ever done that, so I wandered out to check if Charlie was still in his concealed spot and maybe pop open his panel and see what was twisting his gears this time. All the while I was hoping that it wasn't descending military ships that were showing up on the bots internal radar. I tried not to think of that, even though odds were that was exactly why the robots alarm had activated its remote to warn me.

As I got to the bay area, it was quite dark as there were no forgiving shafts of light stretching in through the bay doors or from the skylights above. It appeared the robot was still in the place where I had left him, but it was hard to tell, so I tromped over the metal grating to activate the solar battery switch to turn on some lights. Just then a cold voice stopped me in my tracks.

"I wouldn't reach for that switch if I were you *Jimmy-boy*." The man's voice was different somehow, but I recognized the nickname. Sarge was there in the dark somewhere, although I couldn't see him. I didn't want to make any sudden moves and let him have a free shot at my expense, so I played it calm; if you can call pissing yourself being calm.

I was a bit too shocked and couldn't think of a damn thing to say. To my right, I heard a shuffle below me on the bay floor and tried to remember if I had set my pulse gun down in the lab, or if it might be in my holster. The damn things were so light you couldn't tell, and I knew if I reached for it, that may very well just be the last thing I would do before he blasted me ...and with my luck, my holster would be empty.

"Where are your friends, Jimmy?" He asked.

I still hesitated, with a few venomous replies hanging on the edge of my tongue. I quickly realized that acting cocky would be a bad choice at the moment, considering I had no idea which way to dodge if he should take a random pop-shot at me. I finally managed to blurt out something, and he probably picked up just how scared I really was.

"Came back to put us on ice, Sarge?" I mumbled.

He gave out a hearty but labored laugh at that remark, which helped me narrow in on his position. Bad move for a trained soldier, unless he was confident he had the full initiative. Sarge wasn't worried in the least, and that fact bothered me.

A shadow in the doorway caught my eye, but it was another figure, and not where I had positioned Sarge in the darkness. The dim runner lights along the railing gave few clues to the multiple forms entering the cargo bay. I raised my hands cautiously and turned towards the bay floor. There were numerous pipes, crane arms and railing mesh to hide behind should worse come to worse. Old style bullets would ricochet like mad in a mess like this, but sonic weapons had a habit of wrapping around their target like an invisible sandbag. You didn't have to be too accurate with a pulse gun, that's what made them so effective.

"I think I would like you to come down from there now," Sarge breathed with casual amusement.

Without much choice, I slowly made my way off the catwalk and down the short stairwell. Sarge stood there in the dark with a dim flare from the floor lights glancing off his silhouette. He was wearing a long ragged trench coat that helped hide the position of his hands. I couldn't tell exactly what kind of gun he had pointed at me, but his posture told me it wasn't an assault rifle.

Some of the other men around him passed in front of the runner lights, and for some reason, I was relieved to see that they weren't the uniforms of Confederation soldiers. They were dressed in crimson armor; what the hell were Raiders doing here with Sarge?

"Brought some friends of your own I see," I tried to say without exposing the lump that had grown in my throat within the last few moments. A thin glisten of lights reflecting off his shaggy face betrayed his smile.

"Ah, well, my chauffeurs are just here ...*uhm*, to collect their tip," he responded with a sudden cough in the middle of his sentence, which made me wonder if he was ill, "Too bad the rover seems destroyed, I could've used that," he added, "but that column of smoke pointed right to your little hidden base here. It was not terribly wise to give your position away with those tire tracks either ...bad move there, Jim." The tone in his voice helped to mimic his condescending disapproval.

An empty metal crate clanged loudly in the dark cargo bay, and I caught Sarge glare irately over his shoulder to see one of the Raiders suddenly backing away from the metal cage he had disturbed as it rattled to the floor. I took that second to pat my holster. Shit! Nothing there, I had left my sidearm somewhere in the lab. All that was in my immediate pocket was the damn remote, so I palmed it. Sarge must have caught my movement even in the dark, for he suddenly took a step forward into the light to center his aim at my chest.

"Don't test me, boy," he threatened with a light growl as he turned his attention back to his accomplice, "Be quiet fools!" He stressed with obvious anger as the man stepped away. Hurried footsteps along the grating immediately turned both our heads in the opposite direction. It was Doc.

"Jim! Where are you?" He called out into the darkness, not having a clue of what he had just walked into. Sarge cautiously turned his eyes towards him, while keeping

Michel Savage

the pistol pointed directly at me.

"Well now, Dr. Brendan, I suggest that you not take another step and do as you are told," Sarge ordered in his usual arrogant tone. One of the convicts pushed aside a loose pipe as he approached the stairway towards Doc, and it clanged to the floor. He shouted at him to halt, but Doc appeared to panic. Perhaps thinking they were all Confederate soldiers who would be lethal company. In the dim illumination of the railing lights, I saw Doc pull something shiny out from under his coat. He had my handgun in his grip.

"That was a bad choice, Doctor…" Sarge stated coldly in a low voice as he slowly, but purposefully, turned his aim towards the scientist. Doc's attention was centered on the lone convict approaching him up the stairwell and didn't see Sarge below. Apparently, the Raiders were still only armed with their usual ensemble of machete's and makeshift weapons.

It seemed like it all happened in slow motion. Sarge fired twice with deadly accuracy. Doc was knocked one way, then another as the impacts struck him. The startled inmate jumped back as Doc's limp body fell forward and hit the grated platform; the gun he had held dropped and clanked to the floor somewhere below, lost in the darkness. His head lay just on the edge near the railing lights. I could see his broken glasses twisted about his face and a thin trail of blood escaping his lips. There was no question …Doc was dead.

"Nooo," was all that I could manage to whisper, being far too stunned to respond. I was far too exhausted from this whole ordeal, this damned planet, the pompous military pricks, the unpredictable convicts …everything! I suddenly felt physically drained, as if my bones had turned to lead. Sarge spouted off a haughty chuckle of satisfaction and gave a second glance at his handiwork.

"Find the others, but be careful about it, they're armed!" He ordered the henchmen as he turned his attention back towards me, "…And try not to kill anyone just yet, I *really* want to savor this."

My blood started to boil just then, and unconsciously, I hit the channel button on the remote I had hidden in my palm. The cuffs of my coat were generous enough so that he couldn't tell the awkward position of my hand.

"Come forward," I spoke casually as I held the button depressed, then released. I didn't know what the hell I had planned; it was like my subconscious had some wild scheme in the works without the polite consideration of letting me be fully aware of my own actions. Sarge just tilted his head in slight confusion.

"Being the brave hero now, are we? Just what is on your mind Jimmy-boy?" Sarge smirked again as he took another curious step forward. Something rattled slightly behind him, but he didn't bother to investigate the source of the noise.

"I told you morons to keep quiet," he spat out as he turned his head slightly, but refused to take his eyes and his aim off of me. He hadn't noticed that the other men, perhaps three that I had counted, had already left the bay. I caught a flash of movement behind Sarge out of the corner of my eye but I didn't dare look, lest he suspect.

"You arrogant son-of-a-bitch! *Urk*!" I blared as he nailed me with a sudden kick that took me off guard. Sarge was a powerful man, and his foot to my gut knocked the wind out of me as I fell to the floor. I came real close to dropping the damn remote but had clutched onto it out of sheer pain. I looked up at him as I tried to catch my breath.

"Oh come on, where's your respect for your superior officers, Jimbo? Tell you what; I've got a special treat for you, Jimmy. I'm gonna put down each and every one of your pals right here in front of you as you watch, and then I'm gonna slice you open, and keep whittling on you until you look like *this*, you little cockroach!" He spat out with cold finality in his blighted voice as he took another step forward to kick me while I was down. He tore open his shirt; but even in the dim light, I could catch the hint of a horrible scar running up his torso and across his neck. I wasn't too happy to be me just then.

A hulking form hovered immediately behind him as it rattled slightly for a brief moment. Sarge seemed far too riled to bother with the incompetent guards whom he assumed were still running about making more noise than he had wished. I recoiled involuntarily as he made another feint to kick me with his heavy boots, but he faltered at the last second.

"Think you had me out of your way with that cute trick you pulled with the transport, huh? Well, your little prank backfired," his temper began to flare up again, as he gave out a hoarse cough, "Thanks to you Jimmy-boy, I'm here to enjoy this precious little moment together, and as you can see, I'm still alive and kicking!" He finished with a strained laugh while he delivered another swift boot to my ribs.

I turned over on my side as I curled up in pain, but that also brought the remote in my hand closer to my face.

"Well Sarge, you old rat," I struggled to mutter, "can't you just let bygones be bygones, and extend your arm in friendship, ole' pal?" I barely managed to respond while clicking the button on the remote as I mentioned three specific words.   Sarge almost roared with laughter in response, but caught himself and almost choked on his own breath as I rolled over to face him. He was still waving the gun at me as he gained control of his character. He was certainly enjoying his revenge.

"You're a real piece of work Jimmy-boy," he chortled, "it's too bad you're such a half-wit, I could really make a hobby out of you!"

"The Earth counsel would have you arrested and convicted to life on this frozen rock if they knew what you did," I tried to delay, "and Charlie would have you court-martialed," I added in for flavor; depressing the button on the remote as I spoke the name. The grin on Sarge's face grew from ear to ear as he lowered the gun casually to his side, as he was quite confident I wasn't going anywhere at the moment in my current condition.

"*Ahh* …you fool!" He sprouted with a pompous tone, "It was Brigadier Charles who sent me on this mission, with orders to leave your sorry asses to rot on this frozen ball of ice."

"…I know," I stated coldly, slowly lifting my eyes to glare at him. My answer obviously took him a bit off guard, for the expression on his face went flat. I had known more than he had originally thought, and he didn't seem to like the sudden realization of that.

I could barely see the metal outline of the robot stationed behind him; its long probing arm had extended away from its body directly above where Sarge stood. My prospects looked pretty slim at the moment, but I wasn't about to let that bastard have the last laugh.

"The military has twisted your mind, Sergeant Roland; we should analyze that head of yours," I barked aloud as I clicked the remote on a specific note.

A glazed look of arrogance washed across Sarge's face the moment before a piercing glow of blue light erupted directly above his head. He spun like a cat and took a quick plug at the droid, but the shot barely jolted the robot, which had taken my selective verbal commands to the letter. Sarge took a curious glance up at the ball of plasma forming at the tip of the probe positioned directly above his head, as though he was wondering what he was seeing. I propped myself up while trying to crawl away from him.

"You ...you deserve this," I blurted out at him just before a blinding arc of electricity flashed over Sarge from the probe. His body jolted back and forth like a rag doll, somehow being held up by some force not of his own will. A mixed stench of ozone and burning flesh came off him in thick strings of smoke. Suddenly, his body twisted to face me, and I could see nothing but the whites of his eyes as they were rolled back up into his head; they glowed eerily with the erratic jolts of energy that surged through his corpse.

The electricity danced across his body, leaving puffs of smoke wherever they touched his heavy coat and exposed flesh. I sat mesmerized as gouts of deep red blood streamed from his nose, eyes, and ears, and then began to froth. I couldn't fathom why the discharge was taking so long, so I managed to quietly command Charlie to 'stop' by speaking into the remote. In that moment, the body of Sergeant Roland collapsed to the floor.

"That one was for you, Doc," I whispered solemnly.

Sarge was no more, he had died badly. The gun he held was melted into his hand and the rank odor of his corpse was overbearing. I wasn't in the greatest condition at the moment either, but there were still several Raiders within the building, and they would be on top of me in no time if I didn't find Doc's gun. I had to warn the others.

The whisper of a door cycling open came from above, and I quickly scrambled over to Doc's body. He lay there quietly as if he were asleep …but the soft glazed stare from his face told otherwise. I closed his eyes with one hand, feeling as if something was left unsaid. Hitting the switch for the lights, the fluorescent tubes blinked on and I took a quick spin to survey the bay. It was empty but noted that both of the doors to the adjacent domes were wide open.

The rest of my crew was in the communications room, and Roller was laid out in the lab. I limped back down the stairs and found the sonic pistol lying under the railing, apparently undamaged. Making my way up the stairs again, I heard a female voice scream and the brief muffled sounds of a struggle. Expecting the worst, I glanced down at the power bar on the weapon and dropped the beam setting for narrow close quarters. The sonic blast would be the deadliest in that position, and less likely to harm bystanders you weren't aiming for.

Sneaking around the edge of the door, I found Sarah holding a sonic rifle tightly in her shaking hands. She only gave one quick startled glance in my direction before training the gun back onto the motionless form of one of the Raiders laid sprawled out upon the floor. Min groaned somewhere in the background among several toppled supply boxes. Not knowing exactly what had just transpired, I offered a raised brow towards Sarah.

"You okay there, Sarah?" I asked.

"Uh …yeah, is he dead?" She managed to break between her tightened lips as she stared at the limp man. I started over to help Min up, but he managed to get to his feet on his own. A few cautious pokes with the gun barrel at the body and then braving a feel for a pulse told me this convict wouldn't be recovering. A deep voice from behind startled me.

"Those guards must have followed us back... how many more are in their raiding party?" I spun my head around to see Roller sitting dazed on the table, a large bloodied metal pipe sat in his right hand. Wondering for an awkward moment where he had gotten the weapon, I noticed that one of the table legs was missing. He clumsily checked his bandages and then his head, wobbling as if he was going to faint.

"Whoa ...sat up a little too fast I think," he wheezed for a moment. Walking over to the table to help steady him, I filled him in on the situation. Sarah reluctantly eased her stance over the dead guard and kept a wary eye on the door.

"How many are there?" Roller asked again.

"I don't know really, did only one of them come this way?" I glanced over to Sarah for an answer.

"Yeah, just one," Min quickly replied.

"There are a few more in the complex, but I'm not sure how many," I informed them while shrugging my shoulders, "Sarge showed up with a few of those damn Raiders, there could be more outside; I didn't check." That mention caught Roller's immediate attention.

"Roland! Is he still out there?" The soldier quickly responded while angrily twisting the bloodied pipe in his hands.

"Well ...yeah, he's out there, but the bot pretty much barbecued him," I answered. Not knowing exactly what that meant, Roller flashed me a confused expression shortly followed by a curt nod of satisfaction.

"The door to dome 4 is open; a few might have gone that way looking for us," I warned.

Roller plopped off the table and grabbed for a hefty pulse rifle, and then fumbled around inside the doctor's medical pack to withdraw a mini rotary saw. The tool was most likely used for cutting bone, which was an unpleasant thought. Roller placed both items onto the lab table and he began searing gently through the rifle with it.

"It won't take them much time to search those domes; we've got to corner them there," Roller mentioned while he was operating on the assault rifle.

"What are you doing?" Min came over to see how the big lug was abusing his medical gear.

"Just a little trick I learned as a separatist operative," he trailed off as if he had already said too much. That got us thinking that we might have all been misjudging the huge warrior. Roller had always seemed so self-conscience about others, but had just revealed he had worked with shady characters in his past. If the soldier really was a rebel dissident, he was certainly full of surprises.

He finished cutting the links and filed the edges on the barrel in one swift motion. Roller ordered Min to grab a rifle and head back to the radio room to warn the others.

"Best little screamer I ever banged out, considering the circumstances," he stated while giving a wry smile as he delicately adjusted the settings on the firearm. Roller had effectively cut the bazooka-type gun literally in half. It appeared that he had ruined the expensive weapon. I just gave him an inquisitive look in response.

"Think of it as an old-style sawed-off shotgun," he remarked with smug satisfaction. I had never heard of a reference to a 'screamer' or what it was capable of to that fact, but it must have been highly illegal to own such an altered weapon.

"Brendan ran out there awhile ago …is he keeping an eye on the bay doors?" Sarah asked innocently. I didn't like giving the answer. I felt numb as though someone else was saying the words. All heads turned towards me.

"Doc is dead…" I muttered quietly.

Roller just gave an angry grunt. He seemed different somehow, like something had activated his buttons. We motioned for Sarah to watch the lab door while Min went back for the others with a few spare rifles. Roller and I poked our heads out of the doorway; everything appeared quiet in the cargo bay for the moment.

"Order the robot back over to the door, and we'll use it as a shield," Roller whispered just before we headed into the bay. The big man took a moment to walk over to view poor Brendan's lifeless body and shook his head in remorse.

Charlie lurched into action after I gave the voice command into the remote. The bot moved up the ramp and into the corridor beyond. Roller was moving slowly, being far worse injured than I was, and perhaps still a bit affected by the medication our medic had administered to him. We sure were a sorry sight, and not much in the mood for a fight but we had the advantage now; considering we had the firearms and a thousand-kilo robot that could cook anything within short range. Those Raiders were dead meat.

I had to get a grip on myself and remember that it was actually Sarge who had done the killing. Warning the convicts about the Military seemed to have had no effect, not without them buying our story. At the moment, Roller and I didn't much feel like taking prisoners, which was a bit ironic if you got to thinking about it.

Roller took a quick peek out the bay doors up to the surface, but he was out there long enough to make me worried. Every moment seemed like an hour, but I knew it must have been my nerves. I was so jumpy, I almost blasted him as he poked his head back in out of the darkness.

"There's just one sled ship parked outside and the rover is all smashed to hell!" As he inquired about that, it took me a moment to realize he must not have recalled the accident with the concussion he had suffered.

"Uh, well, that's a long story. Is there anybody up top?" I asked with strained curiosity.

"Not that I could see, now let's take care of our uninvited guests," Roller offered.

Making our way up the ramp, we heard a loud clang and a horrendous scraping sound coming from the hallway beyond. We turned the corner to dome 4 to find the bot edging itself along the wall towards the end of the corridor. My remote was blinking, but I knew I would have to pop open Charlie's panel to see whatever message it was trying to convey. Hugging opposite walls, we followed closely behind Charlie as he made his way into the storage dome. We caught sight of a pair of shadows heading through the door back to dome 5; we had them cornered! Then it hit me like a brick. How the hell had they known the codes to the door panels?

For some reason, the thought of that really bothered me. It must have been the engineer in me that realized I had overlooked some element, something just didn't fit in all of this. Sarge must have been privy to the pass-codes for this complex all along.

There was no time to debate this with Roller, who

cautiously made his way to the edge of the door.   I whispered into the remote and Charlie stopped in his tracks. Beyond, I clearly saw two dark figures moving in the last dome. The manta-sub was still docked on the far side of the room while the monitoring panels continued to blink in silence.

Ordering Charlie to advance into the doorway, we took cover behind the arctic robot. There was a shout as one of the Raiders scurried across the room to hide behind some equipment. At the sight of the huge mechanical droid, his comrade ran across the grating towards the open sub. Roller shouted out from behind the shield of our automaton since Charlie was too large to fit through the last doorway.

"Drop your weapons and come out where we can see you!" Roller shouted. A clang of metal and hushed voices in the background was the only response we got. He turned to me with an aggravated look of disapproval.

Taking a few seconds to think about it, I sure didn't want to activate Charlie's electrical probe anywhere near this room. The weapon would most likely destroy all of the monitoring equipment, and the power surge could possibly fry our entire electrical system for the base and our radio transmitter to boot.

Roller took a quick moment to brief me on his plan of attack, and on his cue, I ordered the bot to twist its upper body sideways while Roller bolted up over its studded tracks and barely squeezed past its metal torso. He fell to the floor accidentally but recovered his stance in one quick motion. I wasn't quite as agile, as I painfully climbed up over the spiked tracks; where I caught my foot in a loose cable and lost my grip on the droids slippery casing. I came crashing to the floor right behind

Roller just as one of the felons charged us, armed with a jagged spear. Roller turned to face our assailant as I was left scrambling for my dropped gun when a painful roar suddenly filled the room, so loud that I had to cover both my ears in head-splitting agony.

It died instantly, but all of the loose pipes and metal in the room continued to ring with a dulled chime. Sitting up among the bundles of wiring on the floor, I could see one convict lying flat on his back, blood oozing from his ears. So, *that's* why it's called a screamer.

There was still another man in the back of the room; apparently, Roller's exotic weapon only had a small effective radius of a few meters. The other guard fumbled with a crude crossbow as he nearly tripped backward over all the thick wires and tubing lining the floor. When Roller ran forward to fire the screamer again, I saw the little wads of cloth he had used to plug his ears, which I had previously failed to notice.

In its altered condition, the screamer ate through its power cell with a vengeance. Its energy bar had already been reduced by a third by that single blast. I was hoping Roller had noticed that fact since he failed to bring a backup sidearm. Apparently he hadn't.

The screamer went off again as he rushed the man. Even at a fair distance, I had to cover my ears because of the pain. The guard faltered, and his shot went high. The bolt pierced a pressurized pipe and a thick vent of steam burst out from the scarred tubing. The convict held one hand to his bleeding ears in obvious agony as he fumbled for a knife with the other. Roller had not gotten close enough for the sonic charge to take out his target. A quick kick at his assailant's hand sent the knife flying, and he blasted the poor fellow again at point-blank. The man's face turned a lurid red as gouts of blood trickled from his ears; his bloodshot eyes froze with a terrible blank stare which displayed the saturated pain he had suffered.

It was just then that something out of the corner of my eye drew my attention, the movement of a shadow near the open sub. Roller caught it too, just as he raised his gun and pulled the trigger. The screamer gave a quiet whir as the power cell died, and Roller gave a nervous glance down at the energy bar. Oh shit.

Turvel stood at the edge of the sub with a quad-barrel assault rifle pointing directly at Roller's head.

"It seems like you weren't bluffing about the downed Confederation ship after all. Too bad for you, that our mutual friend, Mr. Cross, provided a true insight into your presence here," Turvel stated.

"I only tried to warn you, because I thought it might be worth saving your sorry necks; but apparently, not everyone on this rock is worth the trouble. Sorry shit like you belongs here, Turvel!" Roller responded, straining to control his aggravation.

The convict gave a smug laugh, but continuously broke his concentration on us to eye the doorway. He was probably waiting for his comrades, or Sarge; neither of whom would be arriving.

"I own this moon, little man, and everyone on it," Turvel spat in return, "You will do as I say, or pay!"

Roller dropped his useless gun in clear contempt then bent over slowly in apparent defeat. Turvel tilted his head in amused glee and started to open his mouth to say something. In one smooth motion, Roller collapsed to the floor, grabbed the butt of the screamer as he twisted around, and sent the hunk of metal flying like a bolo into

Turvel's face. It was a desperate move that wouldn't have worked, but for one exception.

Startled, Turvel took one step in reverse and tripped over the rim of the manta and fell back into the narrow couch. With his rifle still in hand, he recovered quickly and took aim for the prone soldier. Roller's eyes opened wide, knowing his brains were about to be scrambled into oblivion. In that nanosecond, I slapped the buttons on the console near the door where I had seen Doc standing before. A few of the depressed lights turned green as the shield instantly closed shut on the sub.

Realizing the glass shield had just cocooned him within the chair, Turvel began to bang on the surface in frustration with the butt of his gun. Roller gave a backward glance of surprise towards me as I yelled for him to step away from the tracks. Upon activation, the console lit up in front of the trapped convict. Turvel instantly began depressing buttons in a desperate attempt to release the hatch, so I motioned Roller back towards the door in case he succeeded.

The grating on the floor cycled open with a roar of steam, and the manta edged forward towards the dark pit below. Roller looked on in astonishment, not knowing what to expect. It was over now; Turvel wouldn't get out of the mini-sub in time. His angry face glared at us from behind the shield. I could tell the exact moment when he noticed the chasm in front of him and what was about to happen. A flash of cold terror washed over him as the ship tipped over the edge. I lost sight of Turvel's silent scream as he disappeared into the darkness below.

Roller cautiously peered over the edge into the hole, jumping back as the grating suddenly cycled shut.

"What the hell was that?" He asked timidly.

"A submarine; it goes under the ice to an aquatic base. It's a long story, Roller. I'll have to fill you in about it sometime if the Troopers don't finish us off first," I blurted, glancing over at the screen and watching the blip on the monitor descend down a wire-frame shaft.

"The troopers …oh, the Troopers!" Roller livened up, "When is our rescue ship due to land?" He almost shouted at me in his sudden hysteria, something had apparently provoked his sudden alarm.

"Well, uh, Voc calculated it should be anytime now, we are trying to beat the landing of the military squadrons. We've got to get on that rescue ship; otherwise, we don't stand much of a chance," I finished, but he looked upset at this news.

"We have to warn them not to land!" Roller responded quickly as he headed back towards Charlie, who sat peacefully glaring at us from the doorway. I ordered the robot to backtrack into the storage room so we could get around him.

"But why? We have to get off this snowball ASAP. Our only chance is to outrun the Confederation ships!" I replied, confused until I heard Roller's rattled response.

"Sarge didn't destroy it, the Sentry orbital is still operational!" He barked back.

The sentinel satellite was still ticking? Dammit! If it's not one thing, it's another. Well, so much for our ride home. I thought to myself; *this is hopeless*, and started to feel that twisting knot of desperation in the pit in my stomach again.

Troopers

"What do you mean it's still activated?" I huffed as we ran for the communications room. Roller didn't stop to explain it to me until we reached Rook and Voc, who nearly shoved the muzzles of their pulse rifles down our throats when we barged into the room.

"No more bogies, perimeter secured; all enemy units down," Roller barked out quickly; then realized that what he had just said sounded a bit over the top, considering we weren't bona fide military personnel. He quickly filled in Rook and the rest of us on the situation, and how Sarge had gotten slammed back down onto Europa. This was bad, very bad. There was no way a rescue ship could get to us if we couldn't get those damn sentinel satellites turned off.

"But I don't understand. We all saw the Folder blow up the base," Rook questioned. It was then that we began to remember that the transmission dish had actually been switched to a broadband frequency that might have only scathed or had entirely missed the targeted satellite net with its concentrated electron pulse.

Rook got back on the radio and sent out a frantic mayday to the Phobos mining vessel that was coming for us. Amazingly, the call was returned, as we thought we would not be able to get through so quickly.

"*Krrrtt~* Echo Uniform, we read you; this is Captain Briggins of the Phobos mining corporation. We are attempting to narrow in on your signal and give an ETA of minus three-zero minutes before touchdown., over."

Rook switched bands to relieve the static and she

snatched the data cube that I offered to her out of my hand. Voc set this into a port on the console and hit a few switches to activate the transmitter.

"Negative, Phobos, repeat, Negative!" She repeated slowly, "Do not attempt to land! If you can, hold position beyond outer orbit until further notice, and keep an eye out for any approaching Confederation ships. Turn on your recorders, we are about to send you some vital data. Over."

At that, Voc hit a switch and sent the info on the data cube out on the airwaves into space. This he did on broadband, although the mass of Jupiter was blocking most of the signal to the inner planets, the nearby mining ship would pick it up clearly.

"*Krrrtt~* Echo Uniform, your transmission upload was received from the surface; however, your previous communication was partially broken, please repeat. Our onboard radar shows that there are several Confederation cruisers ahead of us closing in on your position. Do you still need assistance? Over."

Holy shit! Rook gave us a quick worried glance and turned back to the console just as static began to click in and out, then terminated to nothing but dead air.

"Phobos, come in Phobos! Negative, do not attempt to land. Repeat, *do not* attempt to land. Do not engage, and maintain orbit, please confirm, over," She steadily repeated while trying to adjust the frequency. There was no response, nothing; even the dead air sounded unusual. Rook turned to us, referring to the dull sound droning over the speakers.

"It's no use. Apparently, the military cruisers have flooded the channels with feedback and blocked our signal. They must not have liked the information we just sent out over the air," Rook relayed.

Voc and Sarah passed a nervous look as we fiddled with our guns uselessly. It looked like the Troopers were going to arrive first, and our rescue vessel would only get here in time to mop whatever was left of us off the ice. Most likely, the star cruisers would also shoot down the approaching rescue ship just for knowing too much; and we slowly came to the realization we had probably just condemned them by transmitting that data cube. Things quickly began to fall apart, and Sarah started to cry. Hell, I couldn't blame her.

"But wait a minute," Voc broke the silence, "if the Sentry is still up and running, then what will the Confederation do?"

"Most likely they will maintain an armada in orbit around this moon, and there's a high probability that they will atomize any non-military ships in the vicinity," Roller added in response. That got me thinking.

"That is, unless they don't know that the Sentry is still ticking," I added with a wince. The wheels in my head were starting to spin on their own again. I remembered that Sarge had activated the Electron Folder to kill the satellite, which he had failed to do. As a result, he got zapped while attempting to leave orbit and crash-landed. This means that all his equipment also got fried and he had no way to contact the Confederation with an update about the situation. He had simply failed to show at his rendezvous point on Ganymede.

Just then, all of our hand radios began to buzz loudly. Rook hopped up first out of her seat and threw aside her headset in clear aggravation. She tucked her white hair behind her cowl and grabbed a rifle as she headed for the surface.

"They're landing!" Was all she said, with a single cold glance back at us. We all grabbed our guns and headed for the door; it looked like we were in for a fight. There was no way we were going to get out of this alive.

We made it out into the cold night past the smoking remains of the rover to one of the sail-ships parked nearby. The night winds howled and slapped at our ragged clothes. Out of desperation, I headed over to the Raider's sled and took a look at the rigging. I had absolutely no idea how to work the thing, but it was our only mode of transportation at the moment.

Voc came up behind me, also inspecting the strange vehicle. He tossed a handful of jagged spears off the sled and picked up something in a dark corner that had caught his eye. It was Sarge's bag! Min yelled to the rest of us as he pointed to the night sky.

"Look up there!" He shouted.

A large ship sped across the stars above. It was the silhouette of one of the Military cruisers, softly outlined by the dim afterglow of Jupiter. A second ship also appeared several kilometers distant. Having been fairly familiar with the schematics, I knew each carrier held around 2000 well-armed troopers and even up to 3000 personnel if they filled them to the brim. The white surface of Europa was about to turn blood red.

As if hitting a switch, all of the lights on the closest ship flickered for a moment, and then went out. Nothing but a shadow of the dark hulk was left in its wake. Guidance lights, drive burners, armament spotlights …everything on it went pitch black. The silhouette of the star cruiser glided silently over our heads. Then the following ship in the background also blinked out in tandem, leaving nothing but a dark gray shadow crossing the evening sky.

As we looked around, several more Confederation ships appeared over the horizon, and we watched as every one of their lights simultaneously winked out upon approach. Was this some sort of stealth tactic to catch the convicts by surprise? Both Rook and Voc let out a frightened laugh, for they couldn't believe what they were seeing.

It hit me just then. Since they had jammed all of the communications channels to keep us from sending further transmissions, they were unable to monitor each of their own strike ships that had taken point and got systematically fried by the Sentry until it was far too late. The Prof erupted with a haughty giggle as we all stood there stunned. We watched as the first battle cruiser silently glided by as it skimmed the atmosphere, then slowly turned into an uncontrolled dive towards the surface. The wind carried the sound of distant thunder across the tundra, announced by a blue flash as each of the ships crashed, pounding into the hard ice of the frozen moon.

Voc was already mouthing calculations that a good 5% or so of the soldiers might survive the impact, should their spacecraft hit at a lucky angle, but if the convicts had found those weapons from the wreckage of that recon vessel; they would certainly put up a decent fight. Out of nowhere, Voc squeaked loudly.

"Oh no, the rescue ship didn't confirm our message; it probably got blocked out as they were jamming our signal. Our only way off this snowball is about to crash and burn!" He blurted in alarm. Rook reacted to this revelation and they both scrambled off back to the communications room. Those of us who could tear our eyes away from the epic spectacle of the crashing starships, followed the rest of the crew below.

The feedback web the military ships had used to blanket this sector was beginning to break down as each of the cruisers were destroyed. Waves of static were fluctuating intermittently with dead air and a few frantic words mixed within the garble that came over the speaker. There was no way we were going to get through. In minus 20 minutes, the mining shuttle would get toasted as well. Voc fumbled through Sarge's frayed bag, and an idea sparked in his head as he emerged with the useless stellar communicator in his hand.

"Isn't that fried?" Sarah asked while we hurried out of his way as he dove for his tool kit. He didn't even bother to face her with his cool response, as all his attention was on the communicator he was tearing apart.

"Yes and no. The hardware is still here, just the crystals in the vital chips got burned out," as he flashed a serious grin, "but luckily, we have spares."

Repairing this device was something any specialized logistics technician could do. That is, if one had time to focus clearly; without several hysterically screaming crewmates hoarding around you as you worked, while your ship was diving out of control from orbit towards a very sudden and unpleasant death; a scenario that was going on planet-wide across the skies at this very moment. Not a kind thought, but those military bastards certainly deserved it!

There was nothing we could do but to let Voc concentrate on his work. Even when Rook tried to help, he hissed his impatience for her to get out of his way. The technician's personality dramatically changed while under pressure. From his behavior, I would assume he wanted to get off this rock twice as much as anyone else in the group. Scavenging a bundle of wires, which he hastily connected to the console, Voc finally eased up and gave a sigh of relief.

"Are you able to call the ship now?" Sarah inquired impatiently. I closed in on Voc as he double-checked his connections, which were quite fragile. He completely ignored her question and attempted voice contact with the rescue shuttle. When that failed, he typed in a message on its tiny console. No reply came from the ship. However, a short blip of a message rolled across the small screen: <CNTRI:4/JE6 ~ RESPONDING>.

For a brief moment, I caught a look of confusion on Voc's face. Which was an expression of his I had never actually seen before; however, he quickly recovered. A glance at the power bar told us that a strong signal was coming in from the orbiting Sentry.

"Let's try this again, shall we?" Voc offered as he typed in an intricate string of data to bypass the lock-out code. A few short commands to Rook, and they transmitted the shutdown program to the ring of sentry satellites.

Voc almost dropped the damn communicator as it abruptly sparked and something inside it fizzled. The miniature cloud of smoke effectively broke the tense silence in the room as he set the unit delicately onto his lap. We could see the string of data flooding the screen with its ritualistic protocol and procedural codes as the AI brain demanded 'why' it should shut itself down, repeating the same line of garbage we had gotten before.

"Oh god, this is *useless*!" I spat in disgust as I raised my hands in resignation; that some cheap half-credit brain chip of a self-posturing, moody computer was giving us such grief. Voc, on the other hand, silently tilted his head in thought as we all began to erupt with the hopelessness of the situation. Especially since we couldn't get through to our rescue ship, and that cursed Sentry was now blocking the only open channel. Almost unnoticed by us, Voc slowly, but deliberately, typed something into the jerry-rigged console sitting in his lap.

We all hushed our whining abruptly as a row of tiny green lights popped up on all the panels and a communique from the mining ship came over the speaker loud and clear. I gave a quick glance over to Voc, then slowly back down to the screen on the console lying in his lap, which simply read: <ACCEPTED ~ SYSTEM DISENGAGED>. A silly flickering smile crossed his cheeks, like a little kid on Christmas morning who was in the moment of discovering he had gotten *exactly* what he had asked for.

We all burst in shocked laughter as Rook grabbed for the headset. Understandably, the Captain of the mining transport had been a little concerned with the seemingly suicidal actions of the military cruisers. He reported that there were only a few Confederation ships left on radar, and those had abruptly turned back on a heading towards Ganymede.

৪ට෬

Sarah didn't hesitate to start packing our personal supplies while Min helped the Professor, who vainly attempted to cart every single one of his several hundred bacteria cultures he had on stock. The rescue ship was tracing our signal and would be landing at any moment. Voc and I ran outside into the darkness, and we borrowed Sarah's holopen to draw a giant landing mark for the ship onto the surface ice. We managed to make a large 'X' bordered by a very crooked circle, but at this point, I was pretty much sick of being such a perfectionist. When we finished, I finally had a chance to interrogate our computer tech.

"What the hell did you tell that satellite, Voc?" I was astounded that he had managed to shut the thing down successfully, when none of us could have thought of a damn thing before. He just gave that shy grin of his and patted me on the back as we both looked up to see the bulky mining ship above descending in from the stars.

"Well, it kept asking for a determinant for letting us shut it down," he admitted casually, "It was processing all of its data on a level reasoning platform with a generic artificial brain. If you think about it logically, wouldn't you also want a damn good reason if someone asked *you* to shut yourself off?" Voc mentioned as he raised a brow. I gave a quick nod of agreement.

"Of course, the thing only understood binary protocol, and as I had already given it the bypass code, the security authorization for my input data was there, but..." I didn't hesitate to give Voc a sharp but friendly slap to the shoulder, as he was rambling on again. I reminded him to keep it in layman's terms, and he quickly got to the punch line.

"Ah well, in short, I told our orbiting warden that all the prisoners had been, uh ...pardoned."

I looked at him with awe; that was a real gem of an idea. I patted him heartily on the back and let loose a hearty laugh at the top of my lungs.

"Voc, you're unbelievable!"

ROCB

With the Confederation Cruisers on the run, and any of their soldiers that may have survived their crash landing would find themselves in an exceptionally desperate situation of being alone and outnumbered in a vast frozen prison yard full of disgruntled convicts. Especially since the inmates in this particular sector had the chance to arm themselves with the weapons from the reconnaissance ship. All that was left was to get off this desolate ball of ice and back to Earth, and present our hard evidence of their criminal conspiracy to the public, which would spark the global dissolution of the Confederation Council and their century of military rule. It would be a long trip, so I was trying to be realistic about all the things that could go wrong. With my luck, they would.

The cargo vessel was a tarnished mash of metal plates, old thrust tubes, and patched energy cables. Far from the sleek model I could have designed it into, but as it landed, I thought that old mining transport was the most beautiful ship I had ever laid my eyes on.

Bright spotlights cut into the darkness as their ramp lowered and armed miners cautiously edged their way onto the ice. They had reviewed enough of the first transmission from that data cube to know that the Confederation Council was responsible for mass murder. Interstellar miners were a tight-knit group and would honor their fallen comrades. Despite the century that had passed since the incident, they were still a vengeful lot.

The news had traveled fast; their captain had forwarded the transmission by wide-band to every mining colony within range. A few returned the radio message with their own plans of reprisal, to track the battle cruisers back to Ganymede and attempt to trap them in that sector of space. The military starships would be cornered and the corporate vessels would demand their surrender.

It was a risk, especially if they should decide to retaliate since the mining vessels lacked the armaments that modern military star cruisers had. Our best bet was to try political maneuvering to get the Confederate troops to submit, but from what Roller told me of the military upper brass, their administration would try to lie and weasel their way out of this hole, like they've always done. This time, however, I was sure things would end up different.

Captain Briggins, himself, counted up our crew, and we snuck the old Professor on board the ship under the guise of our late Dr. Brendan. They hustled us aboard, and I felt stupid for asking the Captain if we could bring the ice robot along. Without pause, the flat emotionless "*No*" he threw back promptly shut me up in short order. Rook herself seemed relieved and somehow changed. She walked over and gave me a warm gentle kiss, right in front of Sarah. I kind of froze, to say the least. That was certainly unexpected, but I still had to give a worried glance over to Sarah for her reaction, and a hint of what reprisal I might have to suffer as a consequence.

Rook let go of me with a twinkle in her bright eyes, it was a look of sentiment and understanding ...then she promptly stepped over to Roller, then Min, and Voc, giving each of them the same affectionate kiss of appreciation; which kind of threw my ego right out the port window. The Prof was also looking forward to his kiss from the snow maiden; however, with a slight grumble and a feigned smile, he returned the meager friendly handshake she had offered towards him.

The ship began to lift off into the sea of stars. On our way home, Sarah took a moment to approach me with a look of determination on her face. I just rolled my eyes, anticipating the third-degree scolding I was about to receive; but to my utter surprise, she kissed me too, and it wasn't so bad. The best part was that she didn't run off to share her affection with the rest of the crewmen, which told me her feelings towards me were genuine.   Sara stayed beside me, holding my arm with her head leaning upon my shoulder. Feeling appreciated and content, this time, I didn't let go.

The adventure continues
Book 2 of the series

Rebels of Alpha Prime

About the Author

Michel Savage has been devoted to writing throughout his career. If one reads between the lines, they will find his novels revolve around the reminder that we are only borrowing our small place on this planet but for a brief period of time, and to take responsibility for the environment, for one another and all other living creatures with which we share this world. And in doing so, hopefully planting a seed in our conscience of the importance to preserve what is left of the wilds, our untainted woodlands, and ever-dwindling rain forests.

He has had the blessing of sharing his stories and artwork around the globe, and would encourage others not to waste too much of their lives chasing someone else's dreams but to follow their own.

One of the most valuable lessons he has learned in his years is that there are far more important things in life than power and money, such as kindness, compassion, and consideration towards others.

...share that thought if you will.

Enter the Grey Forest
www.**GreyForest**.com

Also by
Michel Savage

Hellbot – Battle Planet

Tranquility was one of those out of the way planets in a system far out of reach from the normal space lanes. Loners, dreamers ...whoever they were, chose to colonize this world. Thirty cycles ago something went terribly wrong. It was rumored their terraformer reactor went critical, and few escaped the chain reaction that clouded the atmosphere with a planet-wide sand storm. A decade of hard labor evaporated overnight. What wasn't buried under the ocean of sand was left to fry under the twin suns. Human explorers began to wander back into the forgotten zone. No one knew of the machines that had evolved, or the war that raged beyond the edge of the universe ...where mankind did not belong.

Forgotten Future

At the edge of the world an impossible relic from the fables of antiquity has risen from the frozen wastelands of Antarctica. Professor Logan and his exploration team rush to investigate this historic find, but this unique discovery puts their lives in peril when they unearth the remnants of a long forgotten civilization left buried beneath the ice.

Within the twisting labyrinths below the melting glaciers they uncover an ancient culture which had perished from a mysterious cataclysm. They soon realize it was a polar shift which had caused their destruction, and our world was presently facing the same fate.

The Shadoworld Series
Shadow of the Sun

On a distant slowly rotating world, Bronze Age tribes must migrate throughout their lives to avoid the long cold death of nightfall. As of late, strange and peculiar events have been deeply troubling the tribal elders; revealing evidence perhaps, that something is lurking on the dark side.

As for a pair of young misfits, the ancient mystery is about to unfold; to reveal their peoples forgotten past, buried deep within the underworld, shrouded in the shadow of the sun.

Shadoworld
Veil of Shadows

Ash was an orphaned street urchin who grew up in the gutters of a desolate medieval city; his bitter youth spent picking pockets and snatching trinkets from the wealthy to survive.

Over the years his art for stealth and sharpened skills had drawn the attention of the Thieves Guild who took him into their folds. Little did they know that the boys tragic past would one day find itself woven within the treacherous schemes of a mysterious spider cult.

As of late, a series of chilling murders had befallen several nobles within the privileged upper districts. Their gruesome deaths had appeared to be centered around an ancient cursed skull, which had recently found its way into the hands of a rich collector. There were few who would trespass upon the strange realms of witchcraft and dark magic ...but a master thief does not fear those who dwell in darkness, for he is one with the shadows.

Shadoworld
Shadows Gate

Asra found himself alone in the middle of the barren sands, unable to remember who he was or how he had gotten there. Saved by a caravan of traveling gypsies, he entered into an exotic world of dancing acrobats, fortune tellers, and mystics who performed their skills for cheering crowds across the desert empires.

However, his destiny would change the day he stumbled upon a forbidden shrine to find a mythical creature entombed beneath its shattered ruins. Promises were whispered and a dark pact was made with the ancient demon; a bond of magic that would lead him on a perilous journey to reveal his forgotten past.

Broken Mirror
Apophis 2029

Hurtling through space was an enormous tumbling rock known as MN4 our astronomers affectionately named after an ancient Egyptian god of destruction. Asteroid Apophis was the talk of the year that every scientific community on Earth was aware of, although its flyby in April 2029 was to be nothing more than a spectacular celestial event; but as warring nations were locked in global conflict, our civilization was unprepared for the devastation that followed in its wake.

Several years after governments fell and society dissolved a ragged pack of survivors stumble upon the buried truth, revealing what circumstances had led to the aftermath that ensued; leaving them to question their struggle to salvage what few splintered shards were left of our world that would forever define mankind's bitter legacy.

7 - The Fall

A strange and unexplained phenomenon led to the fall of civilization. It began on an evening like any other. The Sun had set on another day but by the next morning, humanity realized that there were no more stars in the sky. Somehow, overnight, mankind had become alone in the universe and only an AI program knew why.

Project EVE

In the late 1940s after the 2nd World War, a classified government program was created in order to explore the military use of psychics to gain an advantage for their soldiers during armed conflict. At a remote laboratory in the mountains, a secret compound comprised of several hundred test subjects were trained to enhance their abilities with the goal of achieving the skills of telepathy and mind control.

Assigned to investigate this covert project, Walter Grant found himself entangled in a web of conspiracy and deceit when he discovered that the residents of the colony were being held captive by the scientists who had hidden the ugly truth behind their dangerous experiments.

At the heart of the project was a girl named Eve, whose extraordinary mind held the key, a child who would prove to them why humanity could not handle such power.

Witchwood
The Harvesting

Every day around the world hundreds of people go missing without a trace. Year after year, their numbers add up to millions of lost souls who are never to be seen again; and their numbers keep climbing ...this is where many of them went.

The Faerylands Trilogy
The Grey Forest • Book 1
Soulstorm Keep • Book 2
Sorrowblade • Book 3

Long, long ago the Faerie had roamed free, but for countless centuries now the fey themselves have remained unseen; hidden and withdrawn, shrouded within the boundaries of the Evermore. How they became imprisoned there was a mystery their own elders had forgotten or refused to speak of, and a subject of taboo among the ancients.

The Elvenborn had become a dying race, and now a strange and dreadful blight was encroaching upon their sanctuary. Ivy knew there was something terribly wrong with her world, something unspeakable her kind was hiding from.

The Faerylands were vanishing, and she had to find out why.

Artwork from the Faerylands series
available online

Enter the Grey Forest
www.**GreyForest**.com